THE RED SHOES

Pearl Gray

ISBN: 978-0-9948714-2-8

Cover picture by Samantha Gray
Cover design by Mark Hand Design.
Typeset at SpicaBookDesign (www.spicabookdesign.com)
Printed and bound in Canada by Island Blue Book Printing,
Victoria B.C. (www.islandblue.com)

to my family

Other books by Pearl Gray

Zabel (fiction)

Salt Spring Island: A Place to be (with E. Thorburn) (non-fiction)

Table of Contents

Prudence Howard

Monaco, 1985

Everything seemed stacked against me. Why, you might ask? But probably not. Most people don't care that much about other people. I sound bitter, I know. But I'm just out of a relationship. I sold the jewelry Yves gave me and left Cannes for Monte Carlo where for the past week I've been sitting on this same marina-side bistro chair, working on my novel.

My antagonist, Englishman, Bentley Tyler, remains lifeless, so last night I went to the casino hoping to get some inspiration. I stood outside watching large black cars drop off the usual suspects. Diamonds, real or paste, swimming over the large breasts of thin hipped women escorted by well-tailored men. I decided I didn't want to go in alone, so the next morning I was back at the capacious marina, observing a slightly overweight man who lingered over the *Times* of London while he siped tea on the aft deck of his impressively large yacht. My intention is to use his mannerisms to make Bentley Tyler believable as an arms dealer, fomenting unrest in third world countries, all the while selling poached black rhino horns from his palatial estate in Zimbabwe. I once visited Africa. I saw a dead rhino with its horn gouged out of its head. It made me sick. So I need to finish this book. The real man is clean-shaven but I'm giving Tyler a droopy moustache because I read somewhere men hide behind facial hair.

By the angle of the low November sun I could tell it was now late afternoon and I'd filled up many pages of my wire-bound notebook. I definitely lose track of time when I write. Truth be told, I lose myself in this other world I create and my constantly grasping ego disappears for a while. It's a blessing to be free of the little voice in my head that critiques my every thought and action. Besides, when I don't write, I ache with a longing so strong I swear I will never let anything, I mean *anything*, interfere.

My stomach rumbled, so I pulled one of my last five Euro notes out of my Louis Vuitton knock off and ordered another cappuccino. By not eating regularly I've been able to prolong my stay in Europe. Call it false pride, but working as a chamber maid or bussing tables would be a very last resort, even though being nice to a head chef can always get you a decent meal. But, I'll do it if I need to.

I took off my shoes, the loftiest heels I've ever owned, and massaged my cramped, numb feet until I could feel the blood flowing again to my red varnished toes.

The waiter placed a frothy coffee in front of me with the polished deftness of a well-trained server, turning the cup ever so slightly before he took his hand away. He wore his hair pulled back tightly into a pony tail and I wondered what he would look like naked, with his thick black curls brushing his shoulders. I could see him as a young boy growing up on a farm in Normandy, enamored with the idea of becoming a French waiter, so he could serve blanched leeks like those his father grew with his gnarled, dirt-encrusted fingers. There might be a way, I thought, to make him a minor character in my novel.

I ripped open three packets of brown sugar and stirred them into the cup, as a black, shiny, Aston-Martin pulled softly to a stop at the stern of a yacht. The man who got out was probably in his early sixties. So is Bentley Tyler. Perfect.

Aston-Martin man came around his car and walked toward the restaurant. Of medium height and balding, his head tanned and lightly freckled, he was wearing tailored slacks and a camel-colored cashmere sweater over a brown shirt. He carried his trim body with confidence, like someone used to making decisions.

The waiter delivered a drink to the table next to mine. "Good afternoon, Monsieur Minelli. Can I get you something, sir?"

"Yes, Claude. Bring a cappuccino to the *Angelita, per favore?"*

"Right away, sir."

Mr. Minelli looked down at my table, studying my notebook. I wondered if he, too, was a writer. I reached for my cup just as a woman walked between the Italian and me, bumping my arm.

I jumped up to save my dress, an extravagant purchase, an ice-green silk Valentino knock-off. "Oh, no. My notebook." I dabbed at the page with my napkin. "Damn it."

"Ah, Signora let me help you," Mr. Minelli said, "Claude, get more napkins."

"It's okay. I think I've saved it." I looked up into a face with smooth olive skin and dark, round eyes that seemed free from guile, yet behind the self-assurance there existed some deep pain. I wondered what that was about.

"You are an American, Signora?"

"Canadian. The west coast."

"We should treat our guests better than this," he said in a mellow baritone that reminded me of Rossano Brazzi in my favorite old movie, South Pacific.

The waiter rushed over with a stack of crisp white napkins. "Will there be anything else, Senior Minelli?"

"Yes, Claude. Make that two cappuccinos."

The Italian turned his attention back to me. "Miss...?"

"Howard. Prudence Howard. Pru."

"Ah, Miss Howard, I have just finished an exhausting meeting and it would be my pleasure to share a cappuccino with a lovely visitor."

"That would be most gracious of you...Mr. Minelli, is it?" My luck couldn't have been better. I was going to actually talk to a wealthy yacht owner, instead of just observing from afar. I felt my character deepening already.

"Yes, that is correct. But, please, call me Carlo." He bowed slightly as he stated his name. He had the air of a man who would be at home in a Tuscan villa.

His gallantry didn't surprise me, though. I possess a well-endowed body, one that men want to touch. And to transform my nondescript light brown hair into a sensuous delight I evoke the mantra of the twentieth century – better living through chemistry. Every month I sit at my stylist's while he carefully selects strands of hair, covers them with peroxide, then folds each section into its own piece of aluminum foil. What appears when my hair is shampooed, cut and styled is a sleek, shoulder-length bob. When I'm sitting in an elegant restaurant with my latest romantic interest, the blond strands catch the candlelight and glow, like warm honey. The persona I've developed wraps around me like a finely woven silk scarf. It opens doors.

I remember a conversation I had with my mother. We were drinking tea after a philosophy class I took at university.

"Why did you name me Prudence? It's so Puritan. Why not Catherine?" imagining myself as Czarina of Russia.

My mother had read philosophy, too, being especially interested in Immanuel Kant.

"I hoped it's meaning would favorably influence your life. Prudence is the precondition of all the virtues. How can you be courageous if you don't consider the consequences? Acting rashly would be foolhardy and acting too carefully would be timorous. To be prudent one has to deliberate on what is good or bad in each circumstance."

"No pressure, Mom, thanks," I said as I poured more tea from the brown betty. Just loads of expectations.

I continued to study Kant and found he declared prudence is not a virtue but enlightened or shrewd self-love. And that sounded a bit on the...well, selfish side. The trouble is, in order to write, I need experiences that become fragments of memory to swirl with my imagination, like a twin vortex, until they distill into a creative whole. I was born into the Canadian middle class, and, like I said earlier, it would be prudent of me to meet some men in the upper echelons of wealth and power, so I can make my character, Bentley Tyler, seem real.

I've been in Europe four years and have had two novels published. When I don't have a romantic interest – a man who is prepared to take care of me in the style to which I have become accustomed, as they say – I live off the meager royalties from these novels, but money has a way of slipping through my fingers. As I stated earlier, I'm between men, hence my current dilemma. This new novel I'm working on is my best so far. Once it's published, I'm convinced I'll have some serious money of my own. At thirty, it's quite possibly time to begin looking for 'Mister Right,' but I have to first achieve the success I'm craving. For my long-term happiness, that would be only prudent.

As Carlo took my arm and guided me up the boarding ramp of the *Angelita*, I could feel my luck turning. We settled into chairs on the aft deck which was larger than my hotel room, me savouring the feeling of being one of the elite, wondering what it would be like to own of such a vessel.

I stood my still damp notebook on the table in front of us. "Do you mind if I leave it there while we have coffee. I don't want the pages to stick together."

"But of course. Your notebook is very precious to you, Miss Howard?"

"Yes, I'm writing a novel. These pages are full of scenes I've created. Plus, notes...ideas that are still unformed. If I lose them, they are unlikely to reappear. So, yes. Very precious."

Claude came aboard with the cappuccinos.

"And you? What about you, Mr. Minelli? What do you do?"

"I am a designer of women's shoes. Like you, Miss Howard, I have the unquenchable urge to create."

Minelli. Of course. One of the most acclaimed designers in the world. Only the very rich can afford his shoes. I looked at my feet and suddenly felt like I was wearing two boxes. I should have recognized his name, but he seemed not to be insulted. That was a lucky break. A man with his talent and power could be egotistical, and the afternoon could have ended right there.

I tore open another three packets of brown sugar, stirred them into my cup and took a sip. It seemed like a good idea to change the subject.

"Tell me Mr. Min...I mean, Carlo, what is your feeling about the Common Market? I've been reading Margaret Thatcher's comments in the Times."

"Freeing lorry drivers from endless hours of waiting at border crossings has made an enormous difference in business efficiency, to name but one of the benefits."

"That would be huge, of course. But what about the pressure from Brussels and some of the heads of state who are advocating for a truly federalist European government? Do you think it would work?" I pushed my sunglasses onto the top of my head so he could see that my eyes matched the green of my dress.

"I am an Italian, Miss Howard. I intend to always be an Italian. This talk of uniting various countries with a single currency is nonsense. Europe is a group of unique cultures that have developed over the centuries. Nationalism may be old-fashioned to many, but I, for one, cannot see how union will work. In Italy, our way of producing goods is very different from the Germans, for instance, who are terribly efficient.

"But enough of this political talk, Miss Howard. I want to discuss art, the creative spirit. When did you decide you were a writer?"

"Ah, well...after I completed my degree in English Literature, I moved to Whistler with my parents. They built a small hotel there."

"Whistler, I am not familiar with that name."

"It's a ski resort about an hour and a half north of Vancouver, where I grew up."

"Ah, I see.

"They needed my help and there weren't a lot of other job offers. I took over the front desk duties. There were many slow hours and I had all sorts of ideas rolling around in my head so I started to write them down. I guess I was trying to figure things out. How the world works. That sort of thing. Then I decided to turn my ideas into fiction. As soon as I did that, it was magic. Do you know what I mean, Carlo?"

"If one is lucky enough to discover something one is passionate about. Yes, those of us who have...we are very fortunate. I love the way a woman's foot arches as it settles into a beautifully crafted high heel. It is my joy to create these things. To acknowledge the Madonna in every woman. But, of course, it took me some years to discover that working with leather, with color and design, was my medium."

Carlo passed his hand over the top of his balding pate. "Do you believe in angels, Miss Howard?"

I thought for a moment about his question. But then I remembered, his boat was named *Angelita*. The fashion magazines always comment on the fact that Carlo Minelli isn't married and he's never romantically linked with any of the beautiful models who surround him constantly. What's his story? What's with the sadness I see in his eyes? I decided I might discover the answer if I took his query seriously, even if it was odd from a successful and obviously materialistic man who made money from the very secular business of fashion.

"I don't think so. I believe in what I can perceive through my senses."

"Yes, of course. But permit me to suggest this – you use your imagination and your memory in your writing, do you not?"

"Yes, absolutely."

"These are invisible, no? Have you ever seen a thought?"

I took another sip of coffee. "You're right, Carlo. I see pictures in my head and when it comes to abstract concepts like love or hatred...they are definitely invisible. Basically, none of my thoughts are visible to others until I write them down. If that's what you mean. I've not thought of ...well, my *thoughts* that way before, but I do remember Carl Jung said an angel was a personification of something coming into consciousness from the deep unconscious. Pure intuition, perhaps."

"When I was a boy, my mother told me an angel is a spirit that delivers a thought from God. She believed I would become a priest to serve her God, but as I grew it became clear to both of us that He had given me a different gift. I could draw. So to sanctify my ability, she wanted me to draw angels for His glory. I did so, from my imagination. Eventually, I did not accept this either as my calling, but, I have since come to know that there are angels."

The sea air was becoming cooler. I took my silk shawl out of my bag and wrapped it around my shoulders.

"I have kept you too long, Miss Howard."

Damn, I thought. That was a stupid thing to do. "Not at all, Carlo. I'm enjoying listening to your views."

"I am leaving tomorrow and was planning to have an early evening."

"Well..." I stood up. "I won't keep you."

He stood as well and took my hand, kissing it in the European fashion. "One of my mother's favorite quotes from the Bible was, 'Do not neglect to show hospitality to strangers, for thereby some have entertained angels unawares.' You must do me the honour of accompanying me to dinner. It is not often that I meet a young woman who shares my passion for creativity."

"Dinner sounds like a marvelous idea."

"*Prego.* That is good. But, we must leave right now if we are to enjoy the sunset."

Charles Blackmore

Aruba, 1985

Charles Blackmore parked the rental car in front of his Aruban office and strode inside.

"Rojar, what the hell happened?"

"Heavy seas off the coast of Oregon must have shifted the load. I suspect the crew was careless loading the containers in Vancouver."

Rojar van Heisen was holding a cup of coffee. Blackmore wanted one.

On the flight from London he had been too concerned about his capsized ship and its incumbent losses to eat or drink anything. "Pour me a coffee, Rojar and let's go see her."

The two men walked into the yard where rectangular containers emblazoned with "Blackmore Shipping" were stacked in neat rows. Blackmore could see the ship was no longer listing. A giant crane was off-loading one of the metal boxes. "You saved her, Rojar. Good work." He patted his manager on the shoulder. Charles Blackmore had always been able to count on this man who had worked for him for fifteen years. Blackmore took a sip of the strong coffee. He had been quite sure Rojar would have handled the problem, but he liked to be on hand at any of his two hundred and eleven offices worldwide if there was the possibility of a ship capsizing. It meant he could assess what went wrong, or if, on the other hand, the problem was rectified before he got there, he could give due recognition for a job well done.

"How'd you get here so quickly, Charles? I only informed London six hours ago." He knew there would have been hell to pay if the ship had sunk. Blackmore expected perfection. Rojar liked that about his job at Blackmore Shipping. It had become the fourth largest container shipping company in the world because his boss was hands-on, an entrepreneur who worked to the same exacting standards expected of everyone else in the company.

"I was already in the air. I'm meeting with Carlo Minelli here, tomorrow."

"The shoe designer."

"Yes. We ship exotic Asian wood he uses for shoe heels, to his atelier in Italy. He's had a vacation house on Aruba for some time, but he's recently opened a factory here. He's excited about some new technique he's invented using the skins of the iguana."

Rojar wondered how his boss did it: kept the vast network going and all the while, staying in close touch will his clients. The constant travelling would exhaust a lesser man.

At the Aruban Shores Hotel, the best of the few hotels that slumbered on the miles of pristine beach, Blackmore left the rental car for the valet to park, grabbing his bag and tennis racket.

The tranquil setting would soon end, he mused. Construction, and then tourism, was beginning to replace the jobs lost when the oil refinery west of Oranjestad was shut down. Blackmore smiled at the thought. His containers were delivering the needed materials. Business was up substantially from last year.

The coolness of his suite was a sharp contrast to the hot, humid air outside. When the rainy season passed, the island would again be a hot dry desert. By then, Blackmore would be gone. He liked this weather best.

He opened the chilled Australian chardonnay his secretary always arranged for his arrival, and poured some into a tall Baccarat glass the hotel kept for his exclusive use. He nosed the wine, before he tasted it.

Blackmore methodically rolled up the sleeves of his shirt, and then slid open the door to the shaded balcony. In the lee of the warm wind that blew constantly on the island, he settled into the chaise longue. Holding up the glass, he noted how the amber colour looked against the turquoise of the sea. He would use these colours in a painting he had started last week at his home in London. From the very beginning, as he traveled for business, Blackmore had visited art galleries and museums, and it had given him the urge to create his own small canvasses to which he applied intense jewel-like colors. His paintings were in the style of Matisse because he liked pattern, but more abstract. The hours he spent in his studio distracted him from a wet, grey London so unlike the climate in Edmonton, where he was born and raised.

He took a longer draught of the wine and felt the alcohol curl through his body, relaxing him. A lone pelican floated into view. It dove straight into the water for a fish, not erring in its aim. The bird floated, savouring the catch in its beak before swallowing it. Then the bird's tail swished from side to side with obvious pleasure. Blackmore recognized the delicious sensation. He always felt that way when he completed a deal. There were many such moments.

He stretched his legs. The Concorde from London to New York had been fast, but cramped. First class in the spacious Boeing 737 to Aruba had been more comfortable. He bent to remove his loafers and socks, then rested his head against the back of the chair, letting the warmth of the Caribbean air seep into his body.

A woman walking along the fine sand beach took his attention. She was wearing a white bikini and over her hips she had draped a long white cloth knotted just where her hips swayed. Long blond hair trailed in the slight breeze. Blackmore stood and walked to the railing to get a better look. She reminded him of someone.

Linda Tranor. He'd met Linda in 1965 at Ma-me-o Beach just outside Edmonton. Each Saturday night in the summer he and his friends pooled their money to buy enough beer, which they drank, illegally, while driving to the dance at the lake. The alcohol gave the teenage boys enough courage to ask any girl they considered cute, to dance to the live bands that played all the latest hits.

Blackmore took another sip of wine. Linda Tranor. He remembered that he, Charlie as he was called then, had walked into the darkened dance hall as the band was blasting out "House of the Rising Sun." Barry Allen, their lead singer, could do a perfect imitation of the recording by The Animals. Blackmore looked around at the groups of girls standing along the railing that divided the dance floor from the raised walkway that encircled it. One of them, whose back was to him, had long blond hair that swayed gently as she talked. She was wearing a pair of skintight jeans and a light blue terry-cloth top with sneakers to match. She moved her hands to emphasize what she was saying and he noticed that she had slim, delicate wrists and long fingers, with nails painted a soft pink. Her friends were paying close attention, laughing at intervals.

Blackmore waited until another of the girls began to talk before he ventured over and tapped the blond on the shoulder. He had yet to see her face, but what the heck, he thought, it would only be one dance if she were ugly. But when she turned, very blue eyes, wide with the excitement of telling her story, rested on him. She was far from ugly and for a second Blackmore was tongue-tied. He swallowed and said, “Dance?”

She turned to her friends as if she wanted their approval. They looked him up and down. He was sure of himself in the looks department and he wore Lee Jeans with a madras button-down shirt that all the cool guys wore. One of the other girls giggled, which he hoped was a sign that he had passed.

“Sure.”

The music changed to a slow number so he had no choice but to put his arm around her waist and take her hand. He held her as close as he dared.

“What school do you go to?” He started in with the standard way of becoming acquainted.

“I’m in grade twelve at Harry Ainlay,” she said.

As they continued to move together there was a slow rise of energy as his body reacted to this girl; the smell of her hair, the softness of her hand in his and the dainty way she swung her hips to the pace of the music. His mouth went dry. He was grateful the next dance returned to a fast rock number and they moved to the thunderous beat separately. When the music ended, she didn't walk off the floor or make an excuse to return to her friends, so they danced again. And again. At the end of the evening it was clear she wanted him to take her home. They milled their way with the crowd dispersing to the parked cars.

"Which one's yours?" Linda asked.

"Oh, I'm here with my friends. I don't have a car."

"Oh."

He wasn't quite sure what the "oh" meant, but they'd reached the red Mustang convertible that Bob's dad had given him on his sixteenth birthday.

"Nice car," she said.

Bob and another buddy Steve walked up without girls, then Don and Matt. The guys all piled into the back and Linda and Charlie shared a bucket seat in the front.

As Bob headed the car out of the parking lot, he turned up the radio. It blasted the Beatles into the still night air. They headed for the A&W on Ninth Street as they always did after the dance. Kids who would later deposit the family car in the garage and attempt to slip into bed without waking their parents, went there to sober up on insipid coffee and greasy hamburgers.

Linda was trying to carry on a conversation with Bob and what with the top down, the car travelling at sixty miles an hour and the music blasting from the speakers, she had to lean over the stick shift to speak right into his ear. Blackmore still had his arm around Linda and pulled her back. Linda pushed his arm away. "Don't pull me, I'm talking to Bob."

Blackmore was no expert on male appeal, but he knew he was better looking than Bob who was small in stature. His close-set eyes made him appear less than brilliant. And Blackmore knew his friend was the 'love 'em and leave 'em' type, using his car as bait to lure girls. He would take what he could sexually, and leave them when he became attracted to someone else.

What annoyed Charlie was he was the true blue kind of guy all the girls said they were seeking. But he had one fatal flaw. He had been born to the wrong parents. They weren't rich. He sat back in the bucket seat and let the cool night breeze blow through his hair. Just forget her, he told himself. But as they roared along the dark highway, his fists clenched, his jaw set. He felt inferior. His hands were sticky as the anger coursed through his body.

But as Blackmore returned to the chaise longue on the hotel balcony, he recalled that that was the night he'd made the decision that set the course of his life. He had vowed to correct a design flaw in the universe. He'd find a way to transform Charlie Blackmore into the sophisticated and extremely wealthy Charles Blackmore, a man no woman in her right mind would reject.

Once resolved, he watched for *the* opportunity he was sure would appear. And, to Blackmore's amazement, it did. After his container business began to take off, his mentor, Lord Sidney Pembroke and his wife, Vivian, invited eligible women to their Kent estate for weekends of tennis, bridge, and croquet.

"I say, Charles. What do you think of Miss Cudmore? A rather intelligent young woman. Head screwed on straight and all that," Pembroke said after a set of tennis.

Charles had tasted his gin and tonic and said with a chuckle. "I've got a fortune to build. You know I promised myself I wouldn't stop until I'd achieved my goals."

Pembroke had looked disappointed. "Just don't wait too long, dear boy. Such a lovely woman won't wait forever. I speak from experience when I say that a good wife can be a great asset socially, as well as being good for the soul."

"I can only imagine you are right, sir. I've taken your advice so far and it's proven flawless. I won't ignore you on this either, rest assured."

But what Lord Pembroke didn't know was that Charles had proposed to Cynthia Cudmore and been rejected. She had designs on a title, something Charles did *not* have. He remained polite to all the women he escorted to dinner or played golf with at Sidney and Vivian's course, but he'd resisted getting involved again.

With all the travelling, he eventually had a girl in every port. He reasoned that as long as he didn't promise a relationship or love on a long-term basis, he was free to enjoy their company and have sex. In this last quarter of the twentieth century, women were liberated. They no longer used their virginity as a bargaining chip for marriage. But, to Blackmore's great disgust, when a woman found out he was worth a lot of money, the demands for something permanent started and he would stop seeing her.

He'd thought of his parents' marriage. Traditional. They loved each other. Still. What made their relationship easy was that they'd met when they were both young, before either had any possessions. As they went through life, they were a team; the family assets belonged to both of them because they had built their net worth together—the modest house, the RV, their savings and everything else they owned. It made life easier.

The sun was about to disappear into the sea as Blackmore emptied the wine from his glass. It would be dark instantly. There is no twilight in the tropics. He decided he didn't want to eat alone, so he walked into his suite and picked up the phone.

"Concierge, please."

"Antoine here. How may I help you?"

"Antoine. Charles Blackmore."

"Welcome back, sir."

"Thank you, Antoine. I will require a guest for dinner. Shall we say eight o'clock?"

"Consider it done, sir."

The process of meeting women and dismissing them became distasteful. So Blackmore had stopped dating. The problem became how to satisfy his libido. Sometimes an important result happens from what appears to be randomness of chance. A Titian retrospective at the Tate Gallery tore a hole in the fabric of social convention, allowing Blackmore to slip through. On an elegant canvas, he had discovered the Renaissance courtesan, a way to satisfy his desires, and maintain his personal space without risking the loss of his accumulated wealth if he lived with someone and it didn't work out.

Paid-for-sex eliminated accusations of falseness or of any deceit on his part. It was a contract between him and a woman, who only wanted to be paid for an act she was to perform. He was but one of many wealthy customers who wanted their desires satisfied. The women he chose were beautiful and always elegantly dressed. They had to be able to talk about art and world political events over a gracious dinner. During their time together, he lived the myth of coupling with Isis.

Tonight he wanted to discuss Margaret Thatcher's recent meeting with the new Soviet leader Gorbachov. He wanted to know the woman's take on *glasnost, perestroika* and their implications for the West. Later, in his suite he would painstakingly undress her, make love to her, but he made sure he slept alone. Each woman had been informed by her booking agent that she was to leave after the act was completed. There were to be no complicated or embarrassing scenes in the morning.

Blackmore waited while the maitre d' sat a young couple Blackmore thought looked like newlyweds. He felt a pang of envy he immediately pushed aside.

"Mr. Blackmore. A pleasure to see you again, sir. Your guest is waiting."

Chez Christophe served Lyonaise cuisine, which since the sixteenth century has led French gastronomy. Medallions of beef, savoury chickens and crayfish accompanied with sautéed wild mushrooms and Comte cheese from the foothills of the Alps were prepared by the French chef transplanted to Aruba, using the same time honoured recipes he had perfected in Lyon. Lyonaise ingredients, the quality of which could be acquired nowhere else in the world, were flown in daily.

The comfort of familiarity enveloped Blackmore as he moved past cozy tables covered with burnt orange cloths. Candlelit wall sconces gave the room a warmth that enhanced the superb but always discreet service. The piano player was banging out "All of Me" with the syncopated rhythms he'd learned in the jazz clubs of Chicago.

"Hi, Louis."

"Mr. Blackmore. Good to have you back." Blackmore pulled some bills from the pocket of his sand-colored linen pants and stuffed them into the brandy glass on the polished black surface of the baby grand.

Her back was to him. A mane of black hair, so thick he would be unable to get his fingers through it, fell down bare shoulders that glowed in the flickering candlelight. She was wearing a white silk tank top and sipping the Chateau Gris he had requested. Blackmore slid into the seat across from her.

A pucker at the corner of her mouth broke into a wide smile. Few of her clients were as handsome as this man; gray eyes, dark hair meticulously cut, soft curly hairs on his forearms and more just visible over the top button of his shirt; about thirty-eight she guessed. She wondered if he had made his own money or had inherited it.

The waiter poured the wine. Blackmore took a sip, looking over the glass at this woman. Her skin, a mix of African and Caucasian, the color of cocoa, was tight over prominent cheekbones. He reached out to touch her hand. It had the crude texture of cotton that had been washed many times. Instead of arousal, the feeling left him cold. He removed his hand and leaned back in his chair, pulled an envelope with the agreed upon sum of money from his jacket pocket and slid it toward the woman.

"I'm terribly sorry, miss, but I won't need your services this evening."

She stared at him in disbelief.

"It's nothing you've done. I'll give you a good report, but I've changed my mind." The woman had no way of knowing that it was the touch of her skin. Tactile sensation was Blackmore's fetish. If he didn't like the feel of a woman's skin, he couldn't make love to her.

Prudence Howard

Monaco, 1985

Carlo took my hand to help me down the gangplank. "Do we have far to walk?" I wasn't looking forward to a trek over cobblestones in my high-heels.

"No, no, we won't be walking. I shall take you to one of the best restaurants in all of France. It is a charming little place. In Menton." He pointed behind him. East along the coast. It's the last French town before you re-enter Italy at Ventimiglia."

Did Carlo see me visibly relax before he took my arm and helped me into his Aston-Martin? We sped up the hill, me wondering how the Italians created a race of people who drive everywhere at maniacal speed, weaving in and out of traffic and yet rarely causing accidents. We sailed along green cliffs that looked forever out to sea.

Menton was at sea level, a small town with clusters of Belle Epoch apartment complexes and hotels, that were, Carlo explained to me, not of the same standard as in the other more famous towns along the coast. He brought the car to a stop in front of a whitewashed stucco building on the ocean side of the street. As we entered, the owner, Julian, hugged Carlo and I was introduced. Julian led us to a small terrace edged with a cast iron railing that extended over a fine sand beach. Potted palms separated the tables.

"You are in good time to enjoy a drink before the sun goes down," the owner beamed.

We sat side by side at a small table with a starched white cloth. Napkins, the blue of the sea, contrasted with the large saffron sun that had almost reached the horizon.

"Perhaps you would permit me to order for you. I am familiar with the best dishes."

He was so gallant; something that I couldn't help thinking the harsh Canadian landscape has bred out of our men. With his charming accent and his rather quaint way of using the English language, I would have permitted him almost anything.

"It is my habit to start with a light aperitif. Perhaps a Compari and soda?" He nodded to the attentive Julian who hurried away.

Julian delivered the pomegranate red drink on a silver tray. The candles on the table shone through the small glasses, turning the red liquid to a dark gold. With fine, sensitive fingers Carlo lifted his glass and took a small sip.

I was suddenly aware that I wanted to feel his hands on me. In my experience, older men are sometimes exceptional lovers, able to be patient, proceeding with a softness of touch that produces the most pleasure. Sadly, others become excited too quickly, leaving me unsatisfied and annoyed. I wondered which of these Carlo was. The thought returned: why wasn't he married or living with someone?

Julian approached our table. "The kitchen has just informed me we have taken delivery of some very high quality dark truffles. I know you appreciate very much this delicacy."

"You are right, my friend. They are best in early

winter." Carlo turned to me. "Do you like truffles, Miss Howard? It is somewhat of an acquired taste."

"I have never had the pleasure, but I'd be very interested in trying them." I'd heard of them of course, but the price was so high that they were out of reach of the other men I'd been with.

"*Grazie,* Julian, tell the chef to serve them with the breast of duck. We'll start with the tapenade followed by the leek soup."

Tapenade is definitely not my favorite, but I already said I would eat whatever he chose.

"A wise choice," Julian said before he turned and left us alone.

"You are in for another treat, Miss Howard. Olive oil, as you may know, is the signature-cooking ingredient of the south. In this region there are still many traditional mills. After the first frost, the olives are picked by hand when they are black and ripe. Have you seen the pickers? They shake the trees and rake the branches with special combs so the fruit falls to nets below."

"Yes, I have. But surely not all olives are harvested in such a painstaking way."

"You are correct, only the best oils are still made in this manner. But, most importantly, once the olives are at the mill a stone grinds them to a paste from which the oil is separated."

"Is that what 'cold-pressed' means?" I know what it means, but he seems to be having such a great time explaining everything to me, that I'll just let him talk.

"Yes, exactly. Milling with the patience of times past preserves the flavor. You will see, when Julian mixes the dressing here at the table for our salad that the oil made this way is a dark gold green and extremely flavorful."

The waiter placed a small bowl containing the tapenade in front of us as well as a basket of bread cut into thin rounds. "Julian's chef uses a small black olive that grows close to Nice. Not much flesh on this variety, but a very, how do you say, piquant taste." Carlo picked up the knife and placed a small mound of the olive paste mixed with anchovies and capers on a round of bread and passed it to me. "*Per favore.*"

I rolled the bite around my mouth. I disliked the texture, and it was salty, but naturally so, not like processed food. I swallowed. "It is delicious." Actually, it was the best tapenade I'd ever had.

"We must order some wine. Julian..." Carlo commanded. Bring me the wine list." Carlo prepared another bread round and handed it to me. "I must tell you, Miss Howard, I like to appreciate the wines from the regions where I am traveling."

He took the proffered card and perused it, and then turned back to Julian, "We'll have the Chateau Simone. Bring us the '75. That was the best year, no?"

"Yes, Signor Minelli. It was."

I noticed that Julian referred to Carlo by the Italian honourific. Here on the border with Italy Julian probably spoke both languages and could use whatever to make each guest comfortable.

The wine arrived and once Carlo approved the label, Julian removed the cork with a flourish. He poured a splash into Carlo's glass. Carlo swirled it around, then took a sip, holding the red liquid in his mouth and under his tongue before he swallowed. "*Perfecto.*" He motioned for my glass to be filled.

"Notice the flavors, Miss Howard, if I may be so bold to suggest. Here, you will see, the wine takes on the character of the sun-baked pines, as well as the thyme and the lavender that grow wild on these rocky hills." He waved his hand to encompass the area we could see from the veranda just as the sun was dipping into the Mediterranean.

I nosed the wine after swilling it about in my glass. I held a sip in my mouth and it did, indeed, evoke the flavor of the local herbs. After I swallowed I was sure I could smell the burnt scent of a pine forest baking in the hot sun. Was this just the power of suggestion or was it true. Who cared? It was fantastic.

Julian came to the table. "There will soon be a chill in the air that will interfere with the enjoyment of your meal. Please, follow me inside." He placed our glasses onto a tray and led us to a table near a small clay fireplace, the flames glowing as if we'd brought in the last rays of the sun.

Carlo does know about charming places. Unassuming, but everything's perfect. I wonder if he was born into money? "Carlo, tell me what led you to shoe design instead of art?"

"My father wanted me to work on our farm, but my mother would not allow it. 'Do you want him to ruin his hands?' she would say. So my father would take his rough and calloused fingers out to the fields to do the labor himself. I was young, too young to feel any guilt as I sat with my pencils and made pictures from my imagination of every angel and saint my mother knew."

"Were you the only son?"

"The only surviving son of the six children my mother bore. My sisters, three of them, are older. Married. Eventually I was the only child left at the farm. It was a hard life. Just before the war. Much privation."

"Oh, I'm sorry." This sort of poverty can be the motivation for my arms dealer to make money any way he can. Maybe I did do something great in my last life. I might get my character to gel after all.

The waiter brought two bowls of leek soup, with a sauce made of basil, garlic, grated Parmesan cheese and, of course, olive oil that he spooned into our bowls. We finished the bottle of wine and Carlo ordered another.

"Finally the day came when I went to Milan to be apprenticed to a painting master. There I learned the craft as it was taught in ancient times, laboriously grinding pigments even though we could buy industrially made paints from the art supply store in the piazza."

"It sounds so sensuous, Carlo, making color from the earth. Intriguing."

"Most of the students hated this. They wanted to get on with the job of painting masterpieces. My nature was different. Maybe it was all those days of drawing angel after angel for my mother, but I was used to waiting for my pleasure. Waiting and longing. It was the longing, I have come to believe, that infused my colors. The professor said they had the sweetness of angels and I would humbly lower my head, knowing why. As I ground and worked with each rock, extracting the pigment, I would think of Michelangelo and the patience he had to paint the Sistine ceiling. What imagination, what meditation it would have taken. I would do something as grand some day."

"You have no idea how romantic Italy, with its ancient ways, seem to me. I envy you your heritage."

"Some of my countrymen do not appreciate the old ways, Miss Howard. But I share your enthusiasm."

Two waiters carried in the duck course, removing silver warming covers after each plate was carefully placed in front of us. "For instance, look at the manner in which the truffles have been carefully inserted under the crisp breast. The French. They know how to marry tastes, the richness of the duck with the intensity of the truffles. It is a custom well worth preserving, no?"

I took a bite and let the tastes linger in my mouth. "Yes, Carlo, I don't think I have ever eaten anything quite as delicious. Now, please continue your story."

"Ah, yes. Where was I?" He washed down his food with a large draught of wine. "One day a letter came. It was in my father's rough hand. 'Carlo', he wrote, 'it is about your mother. It was sudden. I came in from the field for lunch and there she was, slumped over the beans she had been slicing. It was her heart. It just gave out. I buried her. I couldn't wait for you to come home on your summer break. And she wouldn't have wanted you to leave your studies.'

"By the time I returned to my village, he was gone, too. The neighbor buried him and because he didn't want to intrude into my parents' private things he had not looked for my address. 'I knew you'd be home eventually,' he'd said."

"Oh, Carlo. How horrible. Two parents in such a short space of time. And your mother. She believed in you. Encouraged you. It must have been hard." Both of my parents are alive. I literally can't imagine my life without them. That look in his eyes. The sadness. Maybe it's loneliness.

"It was not what you would expect. My reaction. I mourned them, yes, but on the other hand it was as if a fine silk thread had snapped; the thread that held me to the life my mother had envisioned for me. The pressure of her immense expectation was lifted. I am embarrassed to say for the first time in my life I felt free to do whatever I wanted, with my mother no longer looking over my shoulder, hoping her son would glorify her Church."

Julian poured more wine. This is the best meal I'd ever had. But, Carlo seems so intent on telling me his story that he's barely touched his. I decided to let him keep talking, feeling complimented that he would trust such personal information to me.

"What did you do?"

"I wanted to see all the monuments that were the glory of Italy. I arranged to lease the farm to my neighbor, resigned from the college and carrying only a few paints and a sketchbook, took to the road. I journeyed to Florence, Siena, Rome.

"As I stood in the magnificent cathedrals, gazing at the most wondrous works ever created to the glory of God, I was moved by the abilities of the artists, but I became aware that I didn't believe in my mother's religion any longer. Perhaps I never had. With that realization I wondered what I was good for, a boy who could draw angels from his imagination? I was sure no one else believed in angels any more either. I felt lost, alone, in a very deep way. All my ambition came to a standstill."

He smiled at me across the table. His pain seemed real, not a story he was reciting for effect.

"I kept moving south. In Naples my money ran out. I would be getting no more rent money from the farm until after the harvest, so I found work in a shoe factory where I was taught to make thick wooden heels to which we, the others at my workbench and I, attached stiff black leather."

Our plates were cleared and Julian refreshed our glasses. Carlo leaned back in his chair, running his hand over his tanned head. "You know Miss Howard, each morning I walked to that factory through the market where the smell of fresh baked bread reminded me of my mornings on the farm. I would wonder if I should leave this bleak place and return to my roots. But my mother had ensured my disdain for working the land with my own hands. I was full of pride I hadn't the right to. I wouldn't admit defeat.

"I'd eat some bread and watch the women buying fresh fish. They carried it, along with the fresh vegetables for the mid-day meal, in large wicker baskets. They all wore the sturdy black shoes I made in the factory. Their legs were covered with thick black stockings under thick wool skirts. Large breasts that had nourished many children were covered in black knitted sweaters and coarse wool jackets. Is this what happened to the pretty young girls who were laughing and skipping so joyfully on their way to school? Did we men marry these girls and turn them into women only a son could love?

"Naples was a rude place in which I knew I did not want to stay. So I ate sparingly in order to save. Soon I had enough money to take a bus to Messina, then the ferry to Sicily. To Taormina. Have you been there, Miss Howard?"

"No, but I've heard it's quite lovely."

"Yes, the town clings to the steep slope of Mt. Etna, with magnificent views of the sea and the air is fragrant with the smell of lemon. I found a job clearing tables in the restaurant of a very expensive hotel. It quickened my desire for the opulence money provides.

"It was there I met a girl named Rosa. After work she and I would walk with her chaperone. In a similar manner to the wives in Naples, she pushed her feet into stiff sandals with high heels. I saw hard corns had formed where her tender skin met the hard leather so familiar to me. I decided I would make her a pair of shoes that would not cause these problems. I confided in the chaperone so I could learn her shoe size. Then I made my drawings, paying special attention to the shape and proportion. But my problem was, instead of the hard leather used in Naples, I wanted something softer.

"Fortune smiled on me, Miss Howard. One day while my friend Renaldo and I were busy in the kitchen of the hotel, he asked if I could help him after work. He lived on a near-by farm. One of the new calves had been put down after it got caught in a ravine and had broken its leg. A local craftsman who made soft leather gloves that were sought after throughout all of Italy had bought it. We were to deliver the calf in a large wheelbarrow. I agreed to help.

"With much effort we soon arrived at a small plaster and timber cottage. I shall never forget that place. Whitewashed with pine shutters and a beautiful, carefully crafted wooden gate that opened onto a small herb garden adjacent to the workshop."

Carlo poured us more wine and ordered dessert. How many glasses have I had? Well, when you've missed a few meals, like I have lately, you just go with the flow.

"The glove-maker sat surrounded by stacks of the softest leathers. On a large table under a window, glass containers held his dyes. I talked to him of the pigments he painstakingly created in the manner I had learned in art school, and of how he infused the skins with these dyes. Renaldo, who had heard it all before, kept hinting we should go. But I wouldn't leave. I was in love with the place, the combination of the skins and the colors. They say every artist must find his medium. I had just found mine." Carlo stopped talking and finished his wine, pouring more.

"What happened? Did the shoes fit Rosa? She must have been ecstatic. Custom-made shoes. That's very special."

"Yes, they fit her perfectly. However, it was a mistake to make them for her."

"Why?"

"With the gift came the expectation we would marry and sadly, it wasn't to be. I did not think of her in that way. When she realized there was to be no wedding, she returned the shoes to me." He paused as if deciding what he should say.

"She was a nice girl, but not the one for me. Nevertheless, I thank her every day for setting me on the correct road. She was an angel with a special message, perhaps, Miss Howard?"

"Perhaps."

The wine was having its effect on me. I hardly noticed the salad or the cheese plate that followed, the candied orange tart and espresso or the drive back to Monte Carlo. But I remembered Carlo's story with one important part left unexplained. If Rosa started him on his path, who is Angelita? He said he didn't believe in the Church anymore, so what's with all the talk about angels? My novelist's mind was working overtime.

When I awoke my head was pounding. *White pleated curtains over portholes.* There was daylight and I was on a boat...fully clothed, and covered with a Merino wool shawl the turquoise of a warm sea. *I hope I didn't make a fool of myself last night.* The end of the evening was decidedly a mystery.

I could hear water lapping softly against the side of the boat and the lines were squeaking. We were still tied up. I was lying on a thick down coverlet in a luxurious stateroom with plush white carpets, polished teak cabinets and pot lights that were positioned so the occupant could read in bed.

When I sat up my head throbbed harder. I could hear opera music being played on deck, luckily too far away to add to my pain.

There was a gentle knock on the door, and a maid entered, discreetly looking away as she deposited a tray with croissant, butter and filtered coffee on the table in the corner of the room. *Servants. I've lived with three men, all with great cash flow, but none had the means to afford servants.* Beside the tray she left a bag, the kind you would get if you were shopping at one of those obscenely expensive boutiques catering to the moneyed classes all over Europe. After she left, I pulled apart the gold ties and found a finely knit Italian V-neck sweater, red, with long sleeves, and a white skirt with three flounced layers. My size. He *was* paying attention. In the bottom was a pair of red shoes with four-inch heels carved from wood. The name of Carlo's atelier was printed on the in-step in gold.

I ate and then showered. Usually I meditate each morning before facing the world, but decided today to skip my ritual. I dressed in the new clothes and slipped my feet into the shoes. They fit perfectly, not bending my feet in the wrong place like my other pair. They were made from a finely patterned reptile skin intricately dyed to show off the scales. I felt deliciously feminine; the thin straps cradled my foot, almost as if it was being held by Carlo's hand. I put on my sunglasses and, feeling as sexy as Sophia Loren, headed for the salon.

Carlo was outside on the aft deck, a phone in his hand, talking a mile a minute in Italian. I waved and stayed inside, pouring myself another coffee from a decanter on the bar, discreetly watching him as I leafed through the pages of a fashion magazine. He was clearly angry, his scowl visible through the glass doors. *I suppose that happens when you own a large corporation. I just bet things go wrong all the time.*

Carlo slammed the phone down. He pushed a button to activate the sliding door and entered the salon. He was wearing tan slacks of the finest wool, and a dark brown linen shirt. The open buttons revealed a mat of thick graying chest hair.

"*Mi scusi.* Please excuse my bad manners, Miss Howard. I had to complete a business call."

"Oh, I'm the one who needs to apologize. I can't even remember the drive home. That wine, the after dinner drinks...I hope I didn't make a fool of myself." *I rarely over indulge. Especially with men I have just met. It's dangerous.*

"I had no idea where you are staying, so I felt it best if you remained here. I am the one who needs to apologize for not keeping track of how much wine we consumed. You trusted me to order for you. It is entirely my fault." He poured himself a coffee at the bar. "I hope the breakfast and coffee were agreeable."

"Immensely. You have been very thoughtful, like most Europeans. There is such a genteel atmosphere here. It supports one's creativity, don't you think?" I asked, but I could tell Carlo wasn't listening. He kept pushing his fingers over his head as if through the action, some solution to the problem he was confronting would occur to him. If I kept talking to him, I thought he might tell me what was going on. Perhaps I could gain some insight into how he ran his empire. All in the name of research for my book.

"Oh, and thank you for the loan of these clothes. I'll return them to you after they're laundered. And the shoes, of course. They are extremely comfortable ...well, I'm sure you've heard this countless times, they make me feel exquisitely feminine. No wonder you're so successful, so obviously successful, " I said, feeling awkward as I waved my hand, indicating the opulence of his boat.

He chuckled. "*Mille grazie*, Miss Howard. It is hard to hide success when one is able to buy the finest of luxuries. Do not be embarrassed. I buy these things to be noticed, after all. And the clothes are for you. I thought you would like to have some fresh things to put on this morning so I sent the maid to purchase them. Please consider it a small gift for sharing the beautiful sunset with me. When you have finished your coffee, I'll have the driver take you to your hotel."

My hotel. So I'm being dismissed. Just when the plot is getting interesting.

The steward approached to inform Carlo he had another call. He excused himself, bowing slightly as he went out to the deck closing the door behind him. I wondered if it was the same caller because he was shouting again, waving his free hand in the air.

He returned to the salon looking completely ruffled. Obviously these phone calls were full of some kind of bad news. It was hard to imagine anything could go that wrong for someone like him.

I was about to speak when Carlo said, "Miss Prudence Howard, I have a proposition for you. You are a writer, no?"

"Yes."

"You see, my advertising agency has greatly disappointed me." He took a large drink of the coffee he'd poured. "One of their staff was to accompany me to Aruba this afternoon. The shoes you are wearing are of a new material, the skin of a reptile called a Green Iguana. He was to create an ad that will appear in the fashion magazines and most highly regarded newspapers for the spring season. Now they tell me there was a mix-up and no one is available. A mix-up." His voice began to rise again and he paced around the salon. "I am their most important client, by far the most important, and they forget to arrange this. It is impossible for me *not* to be represented in those magazines. My clients expect to see my name in print."

"Would it matter that much if you missed one season?" I ventured. "Anyone who can afford them buys your shoes."

"Ah. I can see you do not understand what it means to produce shoes for the very discerning. In my atelier, we make shoes with the hand, in the traditional Italian way, for those who can afford to pay for articles of the finest quality. The finest houses producing the finest quality. It is the Italian way, Miss Howard." He stopped pacing and stood directly in front of me. "These trousers I am wearing." He grabbed the cloth that hung around his thigh with his thumb and first finger and rubbed it lovingly together. "Here, feel it."

I touched the loose-fitting trousers and the wool was as smooth as silk.

"I can sit in them for hours and when I stand, they will look as fresh and tailored as they do at this moment. This fabric was woven by the Barbera family in a small mill not far from my workshop in Milano. Three generations of Barberas have labored under exacting standards." He rubbed the fiber again. "Have you any idea the care that goes into the creation of this wool?"

I wasn't sure if I was supposed to answer at this point but I mumbled a "no".

"After this yarn is spun, Miss Howard," he sighed, having regained some of his composure. "After it is spun," he repeated, "the yarn is wound on spools and packed into wooden crates. The crates are stored for six months. Six months, Miss Howard." He began to get excited again. "In an underground cavern. Under the floor of that very special cave runs a creek. The patriarch of the Barbera family discovered the benefit of that cavern quite by accident. In the cave, the yarn is kept naturally cool and humid, absorbing moisture. 'Nobilizing the fabric,' they call it. It is why these trousers don't wrinkle when I wear them. There is pride in taking that kind of time to make a quality product. It is what we Italians do. We spare no expense to produce a noble product.

"At Minelli Shoes a handful of workers...they are family, really... prepare the skins to my exacting standards. Then others construct the shoes by hand, carve the heels from the wood of exotic Asian trees." Carlo walked to the bar and poured himself ice water. He took a long drink.

"But what you may not understand, Miss Howard, is the reason I and other ateliers like the Barbera family place advertising in the best fashion magazines. We do not do so to increase our market share. We place the advertising so our clients can see the name of their beloved purchases in print. Barbera suits or Minelli shoes are in a class above. Only the extremely wealthy can afford them. You see, these people recognize each other by the quality of the clothing and accessories they wear. These things are not a status symbol as the vulgar claim. The extremely wealthy have no need of such devices. They simply are signs with which to recognize each other. But the advertising is essential. "

I suddenly knew I was out of my league.

"Miss Howard, my proposal is a simple one. You are a writer. You told me last night that you are here with limited funds, but you find the European environment conducive to your craft. That is so, is it not?"

"Yes, very true."

"I wish to hire you. You will accompany me to Aruba where you will create an idea. I will pay you, in advance, enough to enable you to return to Europe and finish your book."

"Creative ad copy? That's not the kind of writing I do."

"Do not let that concern you. I have found the best ideas often come from people who have not learned to be clever in the advertising field. Aruba is an undiscovered paradise. Beautiful beaches that are mostly empty. We will spend some time. You will get the feel of the place. You will have time for your imagination to roam freely."

An ad for the European fashion magazines promoting a new product for one of the finest shoe ateliers in

Italy, that was quite an opportunity, but for once, it seemed beyond my ability. And I don't admit that often. "I don't feel entirely sure I could produce something that would be to your exacting standards." But he did seem to be coming out of his rage.

"Just come up with an idea. I will have the agency do the final work-ups. Even those bumbling fools are capable of that." He stared directly into my eyes. " In fact, the more I think of it, the more I am sure you will come up with something fresh, interesting."

There were two advantages: he was prepared to pay me, up front, a sum of money that would give me time to finish my book, and in Aruba, I would be able to experience the life style of this very wealthy man.

"And please understand, this is purely a business transaction. I am asking you to travel with me because you need to see Aruba. You need to see how we work with the skins. I am expecting nothing but your idea. Nothing, do you understand?"

I did. He meant I didn't have to sleep with him to complete the deal. But, I realized even though he was so much older, I found him very attractive. In the warm, dry air of Aruba maybe I could get him to change his mind about the sex.

I looked into Carlo's eyes. "I accept with one caveat. I need time each day to write. I have a publisher who likes my concept and I'm working to a deadline."

"*Grazie,* Miss Howard. And I can assure you that there will be time each day for you to pursue your own work." He bowed slightly toward me. "My driver will take you to your hotel so you can pack your things."

Two hours later the chauffeur placed my bags in the trunk of a long, white limo and I settled into the deep leather seat beside Carlo. He pulled an envelope from his breast pocket and showed me a bank draft for $30,000 US and an airline voucher to cover a ticket anywhere from Aruba, first class.

"It's too much. After all, you don't know if you'll like my idea." When I heard the words come out of my mouth, I was shocked. What happened to the shrewd reasoning a person named Prudence was supposed to evince?

"Part of the reason that my atelier is so successful, Miss Howard, is that I have good intuition about people, and I always act on that intuition. Your Carl Jung speaks of it, does he not?"

Thank goodness I'd had a glass of wine in my room as I packed – 'a little of the hair of the dog' as my father used to say – because my hand was steady as I took the envelope. "What if you're not happy with my work?" I was really having doubts.

"You're simply a paid consultant, Miss Howard. The reason I am paying you all the money 'up front' as you North Americans say, is that I have retained you as I would retain any professional. A lawyer, for instance. Please do not worry about this. I am sure that whatever you envision, I can use."

We sat in the quiet sanctum of the first class lounge, sipping champagne, while we waited for the attendant to inform us our flight was ready to board. Carlo was working on some documents and I, I just sat and soaked up the pleasure of being in the lap of luxury. Three years before I had stood in a long check-in line to fly coach to Europe, shuffling my bags forward as I moved to the kiosk. I remember walking through the first class compartment to my seat, marveling at the expensive clothes and jewelry of the women seated in the first six rows. Now I enjoyed the covetous look from the Alitalia agent as she glanced at my red Minelli's. For once I felt superior to an Italian beauty with thick sleeked-back hair and lovely oval face.

Prudence Howard

Aruba, 1985

Ovelia Steinmetz, Carlo's Aruban office manager, met us at the airport. A woman about my age with a mass of dark, unruly hair, she was wearing a long red cotton dress and a series of silver bangles on her arm that chimed as she moved. From each ear a large silver hoop grazed the top of her bared shoulders. She caught me staring at her beautiful sandals.

"Yes, they're Minelli's. When you work for Carlo, you can buy them at a discount."

Her accent was slightly clipped, guttural. Though her name indicated Dutch heritage, her cocoa skin and long lean look suggested she had a East African mother, Ethiopian, most probably. As far as I was concerned, she was too exotic to be *just* another employee. My instinct said she was Carlo's lover; someone he hid from the gossip columnists.

The driver loaded my scuffed luggage into another stretch limo. Carlo helped me into the car carrying the only item he'd traveled with: a soft leather attaché case. Ovelia followed us in an open Jeep, the kind surfer kids in California covet.

Arched doorways and hipped roofed buildings with curved baroque dormers lined the main street of Oranjestad, facing the port. They reminded me of the Vermeer painting of the city of Delft I'd seen in The Hague years ago, but instead of the austere brick and stone of Holland, these building facades of the tidy colony were colorfully painted wood.

Carlo's villa was on the other side of town, on a lonely section of wide, white-sand beach. It was wooden, two stories surrounded by broad verandas. It was painted a soft lime green with the long arched windows and French doors trimmed a pale yellow. On the ocean side, a small stone wall separated an expanse of lawn, a swimming pool, and a tennis court from the public beach.

We walked up two wide steps to the entrance. The dark wooden planks of the veranda were covered with finely woven sea-grass carpets, giving off a sweet tropical scent. A maid stood expectantly in the entrance hall; a black woman, with deep-set eyes and grey, wiry hair. Her wide hips, under a full white skirt, made her look like a teapot covered by a tea-cozy.

"Welcome home, sir," she said.

"It is good to be back, Rosanne. This is Miss Howard," he said. "Please show her to the east guest room."

Rosanne nodded.

Carlo turned to me. "Miss Howard, Miss Steinmetz and I have some items to discuss, so please take your time to freshen up and relax. The ocean is warm and perfectly safe. You could have a swim and a nap, if you wish, before dinner. Just let Rosanne know if you require a snack or a drink."

My room was a suite; a cozy sitting room with large pistachio-colored oversized chairs set on a Persian carpet intricately patterned with flowers and vines in oranges and gold. Loosely woven silk curtains billowed softly at the open door that led out to the veranda.

In the bedroom a four-poster bed made of fruitwood stained a warm butternut was covered with luxurious white bedding and a gaggle of lacy pillows. Two more oversized white chairs faced a small fireplace at the end of the room. The French doors would afford a magnificent view of the sun rising out of the sea at dawn.

Make a small mental note to order tea in bed for tomorrow, Pru my dear. You have just arrived in paradise.

As if she were reading my mind Rosanne said, "I will get you whatever refreshments you wish now, Miss Howard, then I'll unpack your things."

The thought of someone going through my suitcases felt odd, but I determined it was the habit of the rich to do such things, so I let it be.

After the stuffy air on the plane I did want to be outside. "I'll go for a swim now, Rosanne. Some juice and something light to nibble on when I'm done would be great. Cheese and crackers, perhaps."

"Very good, Miss Howard. I'll set some things out for you beside the pool."

I changed and walked into the afternoon warmth. Small puddles remained on the stone tiles from an earlier rain shower, leaving the air humid and heavy. In the fine wet sand, sharp white coral had become embedded after the tide receded. I cursed the fact that I had no plastic flip-flops. But, the water was deliciously warm, like a tepid bath; unlike the cold ocean I was used to swimming in at home. I paddled about, feeling refreshed. In the distance some tourists were trying rather unsuccessfully to stay upright on windsurfers and I wondered if the steady wind made it more difficult, or if they were new to the sport.

I walked back to the pool. On a wrought iron table, Rosanne had left a covered platter with assorted cheeses, pate, and crackers and a jug of orange juice.

I could get fat living like this. Make another mental note, Pru. Watch yourself. Who was I kidding? I have no will power when it comes to food and drink. I sat on a chaise longue, mesmerized by the waves, trying with some difficulty to find the place of no desire my meditation guru talked about. How easy it would be to get caught up in this lifestyle. If I were in a relationship with Carlo, if I let myself succumb to the desire for easy pleasure, would I abandon my writing? I concentrated on the waves again. For a long time I've wanted success – fame and financial security. Truth be told, no relationship will give me that. I'd never be happy with myself and therefore, never be happy in the long run if I didn't achieve my goals first.

I was thirsty but the juice container was empty. My middle class Canadian upbringing just wouldn't permit me to ring for Rosanne, so I went inside for some water. I stepped into the entrance hall just as Ovelia Steinmetz came storming out of Carlo's office, obviously very upset. She acknowledged me with a small nod of her head, and then ran to her Jeep without saying a word. The scent of Guerlain's *Shalimar* lingered in the hall. Ovelia spent a good deal of money on the most expensive of perfumes.

Not wanting Carlo to realize I'd seen her, I hurried back to my suite to shower and change for dinner. As I stood under the spray soaping my hair with the passion fruit shampoo that had been placed in the bathroom, I thought how different Carlo seemed when he was working.

Damn, all I wanted was to experience his life style for a while and then hasta la vista baby, move on with my life. But, Pru, you bonehead, you didn't do that. Now you're involved. You're working with him.

I wrapped a thick white towel around myself and wandered to the open door. The phone rang.

"Miss Howard. I trust you've had a pleasant afternoon." It was Carlo, as charming as ever. "There will be a dinner guest tonight, a business associate from London. His name is Charles Blackmore. Could you be ready for drinks at six? A bit early, I know, but we don't want to miss the sunset."

This Carlo I like. "Six is perfect."

I was definitely not prepared for Charles Blackmore. I had imagined a pudgy-faced Englishman, like the one I'd been studying on his yacht in Monte Carlo. The sharp angled planes delineating high cheekbones made the man who stood when I entered the room, ruggedly handsome. His bearing was noble like a sublime philosophical idea.

"Ah, Miss Howard. I'd like you to meet my associate, Charles Blackmore." Then he turned to Charles, "And this is the Canadian woman I mentioned. Prudence Howard."

The manicured fingers he graciously extended in greeting, brought to mind the beautifully sculpted hands of Michelangelo's *David*. But I sensed a hard polished veneer. Was it a protection, or a reaction to the thousands of covetous looks he must have received from women who found him attractive?

"A pleasure to meet you, Miss Howard," he said with a very slight British accent.

I sank into the fuchsia and lime green cushions that backed low-slung settees. The room was exotically elegant. Rattan-covered fans slowly circulating the air, hung from dark beams that stretched across the high vaulted ceiling. Huge gilt-edged mirrors brought in light, giving the small, intimate room the illusion of a much bigger space. Beyond the French doors, which were hung with silk the color of the sofas, a soft glow lit the western sky as the sun made its descent into the sea. I was sure it was Carlo who'd considered each detail, like an art director designing a movie set.

I dipped a shrimp into the chili sauce and popped it into my mouth. Even the colors of the appetizers seemed studied – ivory Thai rice wraps with peanut sauce and green melon balls rolled up with the burgundy-coloured proscuitto ham on the low table.

Carlo moved to the drinks cart. With practiced deftness, he poured the gin and tonic with a twist that I'd requested and two Cuba Libras for the men.

Once we'd settled with our drinks Blackmore asked, "Carlo, what impact will the closing of the refinery have on the economy?"

"Besides tourism, this desert island, as you know, has no natural resources. Outside of the iguana, of course. And speaking of which, Miss Howard is here to create my new ad campaign."

"An ad exec are you, Miss Howard?" Blackmore asked.

"Actually I'm a novelist, but Carlo is, as you probably know, very persuasive."

Carlo turned to me and said, "We ship the iguana skins to Milano on Mr. Blackmore's ships."

Ships, plural. Now that's a word worth exploring. If Carlo is tangled up with Miss Steinmetz, why shouldn't I get to know Mr. Blackmore better? He *is* terribly handsome. And I can't see that his being rich would be a detriment to a relationship. "You're in the shipping business, are you, Mr. Blackmore?"

"Charles, please call me Charles. I'm Canadian like you, Miss Howard, so I'm much more informal than a full-blooded Italian." Blackmore tipped his glass to his friend. They were obviously good enough business acquaintances to jest with each other. "And, yes. Container shipping, actually."

"I'm from Vancouver, Charles, well...Whistler. How about you?"

"Edmonton."

"I won't hold that against you," I said, flashing him my biggest smile. "You at least had enough sense to get away from the winters." I picked up a piece of proscuitto and melon. He smiled back and held my gaze longer than necessary. The room got warmer.

"That's, in part, why I left; cold, snowy winters and the skiing is four hours away, unlike your Whistler."

"How did a man raised so far from the sea become involved in shipping?"

"I got a summer job at Lloyd's of London. Back in the early 70s."

"Goodness. How did you manage that? You must have been quite young."

"Lucky. My father went to Britain in 1937 to avoid the depression in Canada. He'd heard the RAF was recruiting."

"So he got caught up in the war right from the beginning, I presume."

"Exactly. He flew with Lord Sidney Pembroke who is what they call a 'name' at Lloyds. After my father moved back to Edmonton with my mother – he'd met her in London – he and Lord Pembroke kept in touch. That's how I got the job. He educated me about the shipping business then helped me finance my first ship. He's been on my Board ever since. I really owe everything to him."

"I bet you worked harder than you're admitting."

Blackmore emptied his rum.

Carlo returned to the drinks table. "Allow me to refresh your drink, Charles. How about you, Miss Howard?"

"Yes, thank you, Carlo." I turned my attention back to Blackmore.

"Lord Pembroke opened many doors for me around the world. My game plan was to focus on small clients in less developed countries. Again my timing was right; in the 70s, the third world was emerging into the global community. I traveled to places too rustic for most people. Unspoiled, you might say. I took the opportunity to ship the materials needed to facilitate tourism. Lots of visitors like primitive on the outside but want all the mod cons in their hotel rooms."

"So you saw all the great places before they became spoiled," I said, as Carlo handed round the drinks. I wondered if Blackmore picked up on the irony of my statement. *Don't let him see your cynical side yet, Pru. He's a ticket to more research as well as being very appealing.*

"I saw the need to move goods efficiently into these burgeoning markets. I won't apologize for that. Perhaps you think that I helped ruin these places, Miss Howard, but it would have happened sooner or later. And it's my view that everyone is hungry for an improved way of life." He picked up a wrap and dipped it into the peanut sauce. "Have you traveled to the third world?"

"I've been to Zimbabwe and Morocco."

He took a sip of his drink. "If you penetrated past the veneer of the exotic, as I'm sure a novelist would, you undoubtedly noticed life in these places is very hard."

"I get your point, Charles. I'm especially uncomfortable with how animals are treated. It makes me thankful for the invention of the internal combustion engine. I'd rather deal with pollution than watch animals abused." I took a drink, feeling awkward. I really didn't want to get on a soapbox with these men, but cruelty to animals is one of my hot buttons.

Blackmore hesitated for a moment before saying, "I couldn't agree more. It's rare that beasts of burden benefit from helping man secure his material comforts."

We stared at each other for a second. *A rich man with a conscience. This is getting better by the moment.* "But please go on. I'd like to know more about how you started your company."

Carlo said, "I must warn you, Charles, that Miss Howard is very good at gathering information. I've told her much of my life story. I think she will add us to her memory and we may show up as characters in her books. Writers, I believe, cannot create in a vacuum."

I could feel myself flushing the color of the proscuitto.

Blackmore said, "So you put real people in your novels?"

"Not exactly. Some writers like to experience different situations and different types of people and use that directly, but I've come to understand the famous saying by Cezanne: Art is life seen through the eyes of a temperament. For me, perceptions I've made, mix with ideas bubbling up from my unconscious mind. I try to extract meaning from those thoughts and write about it."

"You see, Charles, we *could* become characters in her novel," Carlo reaffirmed.

"Don't let me make you gentlemen uncomfortable. Things that go into my consciousness never emerge as they went in. Sometimes I get lucky and what comes out is interesting." I took a sip of my drink. "But it must be true for creating a business as well." I turned back to Blackmore. "There must have been some kismet...some ah-ha moments that led to your success."

I remembered a board game we used to play when I was about ten. I think it was called *Life.* One played for fame, money or love, each player deciding which was the most important of the three. I always picked fame. I figured that if you were famous, money would follow and love, well, love always seemed like the booby prize to me. What I feared was dying without being known. Blackmore seems to have played for money.

Carlo said, "I am interested as well. I don't think I have heard about the inception of your business."

"After I'd been in London for awhile, Lord Pembroke, took me under his wing. I traveled on business for him. Saw conditions in some of these underdeveloped places. I guess the idea of finding a way to help development was gestating in my mind. One day Lord Pembroke informed me that an aging vessel he'd underwritten for years was to be scrapped. I came up with the idea of converting it into a container ship. Pembroke had faith in me, helped me set up the financing. I was soon in business, using my total savings of five thousand pounds for operating capital. My real innovation, though, the idea that really turned the tide for me, was my understanding that the industry needed to become meticulously organized with hubs on every ocean of the world."

Carlo said, "Your idea works brilliantly. And now you own, what is it, fifty-five vessels? You're the fourth largest container shipper in the world, no?"

"I still insist that it has a lot to do with luck. If I'd not got the job at Lloyd's, I would never have had the opportunity to do what I've done. I guess I owe it all to Edward Lloyd."

"How is that?" I said.

"Lloyd's is an interesting set up. Do you know anything about it?"

"Not really."

"Edward Lloyd had a coffeehouse in the late 1600's in Tower Street, London. A group of sailors, merchants, and ship owners regularly met there. Lloyd catered to his nautical clientele with shipping news printed on sheets of paper. The clients would discuss insurance deals among themselves. I learned from Lord Pembroke that Lloyd's is still not a company, but simply a meeting place as of old, where financial risk is spread among multiple financial backers, the names."

"And your Lord Pembroke became one of those people."

"Yes. Because of his long-standing relationship with these people in the industry, he was able to open doors for me. But, I really meant it when I said that I was in the right place at the right time. Lord Pembroke's son, who was just a few years older than me, died in a tragic car crash only a few years before I went to London. In a way, helping me, watching me build a business he could only imagine his son would have been able to do, in some way helped both him and his wife to overcome their grief."

There was an embarrassing silence. I couldn't think of an appropriate response and, I guess, Carlo couldn't either.

Blackmore squeezed the lime into his drink. "One of the side benefits of my business is I've met some really interesting people. Many of my clients have become friends. Like you, Carlo. And Governor Steinmetz."

"Is that a relative of Ovelia's?" I asked, glad that Charles had found another topic of discussion.

"Her father. He passed away a few years ago. Just a great guy. Did you ever meet him, Carlo?"

"No. I did not have the pleasure."

"I located an office in Aruba principally because he agreed to upgrade the port with the cranes necessary for loading and unloading the containers. The deal meant jobs for Arubans. That's how Governor Steinmetz justified the financial outlay to the powers that be, in Holland. For me, because Aruba is near the Panama Canal it meant I had easy access to the two major oceans of the world."

Dinner was announced and we were feted in Carlo's gracious style, the conversation moving from European politics to currency exchange problems.

After we finished eating and Blackmore had left for his hotel, Carlo said, "I've arranged for Ovelia Steinmetz to give you a tour of the leather tanning and dyeing facility tomorrow afternoon. Mr. Blackmore and I will be playing tennis and he'll be staying for dinner, so we won't be able to discuss your initial ideas until the following day."

"I'll be ready after lunch." And, I'd be having another evening with these two very informed and interesting men. I hadn't thought of it before, but they have the same first name; Carlo means Charles in Italian. Both are driven by the need for success and each has made himself into a wealthy man. I wondered what other traits they shared.

Charles Blackmore

Blackmore drove back to his hotel and poured himself another drink. He stretched out on the chaise longue on the balcony, his thoughts drifting to the woman he had just met. Not dazzlingly beautiful, but smart. Personable. And obviously striving for success. It was a combination he'd rarely run into and it was attractive. If she was taking the time away from her writing to work for Carlo she probably needed the money. Starving artist and all that. He wondered if she'd ever been married, if there were kids. She was old enough to have that kind of past. But, as he took a big gulp of the rum and coke, what he couldn't get out of his mind was her intensity. It reminded him of himself and his own hunger for wealth.

He drained his glass and rested his head back thinking about his arrival in London in the summer of 1968. Lord Pembroke had him work on the floor, finding residual buyers for the small amounts of a contract that weren't picked up by the big brokerages.

He'd arrived three days before his appointed meeting with Lord Pembroke so he was sure to be over the jet lag. Through the aunt of a friend he secured a bed and breakfast in Putney. He'd stepped out of the London cab that deposited him in front of a brick row house with a small, neat garden enclosed by a low cast iron fence. Mr. Woolard, a diminutive, balding man in wool pants and a cardigan sweater greeted him at the front door. Together they climbed to the third floor where he was shown into a large room with a double bed, a dresser, a sink and a large table at the expansive window that looked south over the tree-lined street.

"Where can I get dinner?" Charles asked Mr. Woolard.

"Just walk down to the high street and turn left over the bridge. On your right you'll see the Bull and Star, a cozy little pub, that. Mrs. Crosse makes the best deep dish apple pie in London. Spices it with cinnamon. The crust will melt in your mouth. And be sure to have it with clotted cream."

Clotted cream sounded too close to the animal from which it came for his urban taste, but off he went.

He sat at the dark oak bar and ordered bangers and mash having no idea what that was, sipping a pint of ale he was too young to legally drink, in a bar in Alberta. A smile curled his lip. He knew this was the beginning of his life.

When a plate of sausages and mashed potatoes loaded with butter was placed before him he was disappointed. But it was tasty and filling. In the next room a piano sounded and he could hear a woman's deep voice leading the patrons in *It's a Long Way to Tipperary,* a song his father played on the piano. But these were real English voices and real English laughter rising after the tune was finished.

He ordered the apple pie and accepted the clotted cream that melted on the hot crust and ran down the sides of the thick slice. One bite convinced him Mr. Woolard was correct. This was the best pie he'd ever eaten.

Back in his room and feeling grubby after the long day of travelling he decided to have a bath. He took a towel and pajamas and walked down to the second floor. When he turned on the taps only cold water poured into the large footed tub. There was a small contraption mounted beside the tub that had a slot for money. How odd, he thought. At home, his parents house like that of all his friends had a large hot water heater in the basement that was always on, always produced hot water unless his mother had just done a load of wash. He surmised this contraption, he learned later called a geyser, must be the hot water heater and ran back to his room to get coins that looked like they would fit. It worked. The room was soon filled with steam and he lay in the hot water and let the experiences of the day float through his mind. This was the first day of his life-long obsession to discover new places.

The next day he took the Underground into the city. He wanted to be sure where Lloyd's was located, so he would have no problem being on time the following day. Then he wandered the streets with guidebook in hand. The different accents denoting distinctions of class, the brightly colored Carnaby Street clothes in the most outrageous, exaggerated designs, the cars that were driven on the left side of the road, and the red double-decker buses he swung on and off, were to Charles, like food for a starving man; he couldn't get enough.

He ended his day at the British Museum awed by the beauty of the Elgin Marbles, the perfectly articulated figures, like living people, and horses that had been touched by the gods and turned to stone. He felt humbled by the genius he observed. And he felt ignorant. He knew little of the history of the Greeks. Less about art. He promised himself he would travel to Athens one day, to the Parthenon. And he would learn about architecture and paintings.

The next morning he arrived at Lloyd's fifteen minutes ahead of time and asked a mini-skirted receptionist where he might find Lord Pembroke. He was ushered into the presence of a tallish man with a full, graying mustache, who removed the pipe from between his lips before extending his hand in a hearty greeting. "You're the spitting image of your dad," he said, taking in every detail of Charles' face. "Now, let me show you around the place, my boy."

Charles was taken up by the older man's enthusiasm, feeling an instant kinship with this man he had heard his father talk about so often.

Their destination was a large trading floor full of frenzied voices. Men stood waving notepapers, trying to buy up the last bits of a shipping deal. Charles had never seen anything like it, but apparently transactions were successfully completed in this chaotic manner.

As if Lord Pembroke were reading Charles' mind, he said, "I'll have you work with one of the lads until you get the hang of it. It looks a tad more out of control than it is. I did it myself for years, for my father. Learned the business, literally, from the floor up."

Each day after the close of the floor, Pembroke would call Charles into his office and discuss the events of the day, taking the time to answer in great detail all of Charles' questions. Charles proved to be a quick study and he could feel the older man had taken to him.

"I'd like you to come down for the weekend, Charles. We're having a few guests, people you should meet. Just casual, although we do dress for dinner. Do you have a proper jacket?"

Charles was in shock. It hadn't occurred to him that he would be invited to the home of an English lord. But he went.

Over a brandy in Lord Pembroke's book-lined study, he learned that just the year before Pembroke's only son had died in an automobile accident. It had been devastating for him and his wife. They had held so much hope for their boy.

"You remind me of him, Charles. I think it's the underlying confidence and of course your intelligence."

Charles took a sip of his brandy, not knowing how to respond.

"Don't worry, my boy, I'm not trying to make you uncomfortable. My wife and I are grateful you've come into our lives, even if only for the summer. We've missed having a young man about."

The success of that visit had led to other invitations. Charles was soon emulating the peers of the realm in mannerisms and thought, these friends of Lord Pembroke's who were the wealthy, and the privileged, who could trace their ancestry for centuries, who still lived in homes built by their forebears, but who worked in the world of trade and finance in a modern London. Charles laughed when he thought of how intimidated he had been by the nouveau riche families in Edmonton. They were tiny peons in the game of wealth accumulation compared to these men of the English upper classes.

Because of Lord Pembroke, Charles was accepted as if he, too, had been born to money. Mostly he listened and observed. He vowed to make himself one of them in wealth even though he knew he could never really be one of them in status. He sensed correctly that great wealth is *the* great equalizer.

He recalled as the middle of August approached, Pembroke called Charles into his office.

"My boy," he began. "I've been thinking. You're taking a business degree at home, aren't you?"

"Yes, sir. I've completed two years."

"Well, that's fine, fine, Charles. But," Pembroke picked up his pipe and began to fill it with the tobacco from a tin on his desk. "I learned this business from my father, as I told you. About risk. About money and finance. It is a real training ground, more authentic than anything you could learn from a professor or a business manual."

"Yes, sir. I expect you're right about that, sir." Charles held his breath. He had an idea that Lord Pembroke was about to make him some kind of offer and Charles knew whatever it was, he'd accept. He wanted to stay in London and he wanted to be apprenticed to this wealthy, noble man who had become an ersatz father. He would never get another opportunity like this.

And so it was agreed. He was given a raise and more responsibility that he handled with ease. In the way nature adapted all living things to their habitat, he learned to be faultlessly tailored. It began to feel to Charles he'd been born to fit into this aristocratic life, so far removed from his middle-class existence in Canada.

Then one afternoon after the floor closed, Lord Pembroke invited Charles for drinks at his club. Edgar Vandross, another name at Lloyd's, had just arrived. The men were standing in the mahogany paneled foyer waiting for their table to be made ready.

"I've got a line on a Matisse, Sidney. My dealer located it at an estate sale in Provence. It will set me back a bundle. But worth it."

Edgar drained his glass and let it drop onto the tray of a passing waiter. "Another, Winston," he said, and then turned his attention to Charles. "What do you think of Matisse's Moroccan period?"

Charles took a gulp of his gin and tonic to buy himself some time. He had no idea that Matisse had even painted in Morocco; let alone what any of the paintings looked like. "I...I like his earlier work better." Charles stumbled over the words and he could feel the skin around his neck getting warm.

"Really? All those incessant patterns. I think the Moroccan stuff is so much more modern. Simple."

"Now, let the boy have his opinion, Edgar. Everyone knows what an art snob you are." It was Lord Pembroke who spoke and Charles was yet again eternally grateful for the older man. But the embarrassment was not pushed aside. Every spare moment, after that horrible incident, Charles spent in the British Museum or the Tate. Some weekends he went to Paris where he wandered the streets and the galleries, absorbing everything French. He read art history books he bought in the museum bookstores while he supped in the bistros along the Champs-Elysees. In these books he learned the cultural history of Europe and its political and philosophical impact on the rest of the world.

Blackmore rose from the chaise longue and walked into the bedroom, chuckling to himself as he recalled those times. He'd come a long way in fifteen years. As he closed his eyes, the face of Prudence Howard came into his mind, a woman he was sure had similar ambitions to his own. He fell asleep with a smile on his lips.

Prudence Howard

The next morning after my dinner with Carlo and Charles Blackmore, I lay under the palapa soaking up the Caribbean warmth, the constant breeze keeping me from getting too hot. It was early. On the stone wall, an iguana was sunning itself, getting its body temperature up so it could hunt for food. It was a large reptile with an upright, jagged dome on its head. As I watched, it must have become warm enough because it moved swiftly up a large palm tree.

These must be the green iguanas Carlo tans for the shoes. Now, I love animals. We always had a cat or two when I was growing up, so I had to block from my mind the fact the shoes he had given me had once been roaming the island.

At noon I was sitting at the wrought-iron table enjoying a bacon and tomato sandwich, when the iguana reappeared, sat on a tuft of grass, observing my every move. I flung it a piece of tomato wondering if it ate vegetables. It did. With relish. Just like my cats. Mooches.

The maid came over to the table. “Can I get you anything else, Miss Howard?”

“Yes, I’d love more tea and lemon, thank-you.”

Just as I finished speaking I felt the iguana, which had climbed the leg of the wicker chair, brush my arm. I was more startled than afraid as it grabbed a piece of bacon off my plate, before stealing back to the ground and retreating under the bushes planted against the stone wall.

Rosanne and I shared a laugh. Now there was a creature after my own heart. Take what you want when you want it. "Leave the plate, Rosanne. I'll feed him the rest of my sandwich, if he comes back."

"What is it you find so amusing, Miss Howard?" It was Carlo, dressed in sparkling white Fila shirt and shorts that revealed smooth, tanned, well-formed calves. He spun the racket he was holding in the unconscious way good tennis players do as he walked over to the table.

"I was just admiring the chutzpah of your green iguana. He snagged a piece of bacon from my plate." I expected Carlo to find that as amusing as I did, but as he stepped into the sun there was a look of disgust etched on his face.

"Miss Steinmetz will pick you up at three. I believe the colors we chose for the next season are sensational. I hope you will agree."

He made a small bow as if he were a young boy offering his work to a teacher for approval. It was a charming move. Not something I would have expected from such a talented man with all his success.

"Remember, if you have any questions Miss Steinmetz cannot answer, we can discuss them tomorrow. But now, if you will excuse me, I'm about to warm up with my coach before Charles arrives."

"No problem, Carlo." I poured some tea from the Venetian-glass pot Rosanne had placed on the warmer.

Carlo turned and walked down the marble flagstones that led past the swimming pool to the clay tennis court. Soon I heard the distinctive thwack of balls being rallied.

I put my feet up on the padded seat of another chair and sipped the hot brew. I'm a tennis player. I can have two balls in the air at once, so to speak. I'll play Carlo and Charles against each other and see who wins me, or rather, the supreme privilege of sleeping with me. *I plan to stay my own person.*

Now, what to do about Ovelia, I wondered? We could become friends, as much as I befriend any woman. In fact, I've never met a woman, no matter how much she tells you she's your friend, who won't stab you in the back to get ahead. There is no "Old Girls Club". A woman won't help you up the ladder of success. As you climb "your friend" is busy sawing the rungs where your foot's perched, hoping you slip off so the way will be clear for her to rise. It's happened to me.

Still, by being her friend I might learn more about her boss. I'll just have to risk the comparison between her beautiful cocoa-colored skin and my pale complexion that's beginning to turn a patchy reddish hue from the hours I've been spending in the sun.

Just before 3:00 I showered and put on a black sundress with a built-in bra, not too low cut, with a slightly flared skirt, and no underwear. It was too hot to wear panties. I stared at my image in the full-length mirror. The dress looked great with the red Minellis.

Ovelia was exactly on time. She must have Dutch blood in her. I'd always found the Dutch to be as precise as the Germans. Today her hair was pulled back and tied at the nape of her neck with a bright, multi-colored scarf that set off a pure white short-sleeved linen suit belted to accent her slim waist. Gold dangling earrings completed the ensemble. She looked fabulous. *She'll be a real threat if Carlo asks her to stay for dinner, too. I wonder how well she knows Charles Blackmore.*

"How far to the office, Ovelia? Do we have time to get to know each other?" I said as I climbed into the jeep beside her.

"There's not much to tell. I'm a single mother with three boys, six, seven and eight. Besides work, it takes all my energy to keep up with them. Little boys just don't ever seem to need a rest. What about you?"

Well, by the sounds of her life, she couldn't have time to be Carlo's lover. So I wonder what they could have been arguing about yesterday.

"I'm a writer who took this job to get enough money to finish the novel I'm working on. My money was running out and I would have had to take a less exciting job if Carlo hadn't come along. But, he probably told you all that."

Out of the corner of my eye I could see her relax. He *is* important to her, then. As the jeep approached the traffic circle on the east side of town, Ovelia geared down and eased into the traffic. On the waterside I noticed a work yard surrounded by chain-link fence, with a large number of shipping containers stacked in rows. Emblazoned on the sides of the rust-colored boxes was "Blackmore Shipping". Charles' Aruba operation looked efficient and costly; the sort of place that created serious cash flow.

Ovelia followed a road that led away from the water and turned left onto a street of small commercial buildings.

An attempt had been made to soften their utilitarian bleakness by plantings of tall, large leaved hedges along the cinder-block walls. All the windows were barred. We stopped in front of Carlo's factory and walked up a concrete step to the main entrance.

As Ovelia pulled the door open, the sound of Bob Marley singing "One Love" blasted into the otherwise quiet afternoon. Inside there was no reception area, but the reggae beat made the interior feel welcoming. Banks of fluorescent lights hung over work benches.

"This is the most interesting part of the workshop," Ovelia said. "Come this way. I will show you what the staff are doing."

Eight faces turned to look up at us. Ovelia pointed to each person and said his or her name. "I know you won't remember all these new names, but you'll get to know them in time."

"These vats are filled with chromium oxide. The skins move from vat to vat as the tanning proceeds."

On another group of tables were a pile of skins and each person had a tub filled with a different color dye. "Carlo personally mixed each of these colors. This is "disco pink" and this one is "Tuscan gold." She looked down at my shoes. "Those are "red passion.""

"Pulsing" was the word that came to mind to describe these tones; resonant like the passion of the opera music Carlo so loved. *That might be the beginning of an idea for the ads.*

Ovelia said, "When this initial color is applied and dries, the dyers lift the scales of the iguana skin and spray the underside with a darker or contrasting metallic color.

The method Carlo invented for doing this is unique, and as you know, the effect is utterly eye-catching. The line has become so successful in Europe that Carlo is working on designs for some handbags. Something he's not done before. But, you know Carlo, they will be divine."

I had to admit that I couldn't wait to get back to Italy and wear my shoes to a disco. I could dance all night in these puppies and imagined the light from the disco ball reflecting off the lustrous paint as I boogied about the floor with some handsome local.

Ovelia motioned me aside and the team went back to their various tasks. She reached up and checked the state of her hair, looking suddenly awkward and uncomfortable. With lowered voice she asked, "Has Carlo told you about the process of procuring the skins?"

I thought of the green iguana I'd fed at lunch. Remembered it observing me, deciding when the time was right to pilfer my bacon. I hadn't wanted to think about that reptile being put to death to make leather shoes. Right now I wished to be anywhere but on the other side of the closed door we were about to walk through.

"No, he didn't."

Ovelia reached out and put her hand lightly on my arm. That small act joined us in our anxiety. It was evident she didn't want to go through that door either. "You must steal yourself. It is not a pretty sight."

"I'm okay, if you're okay."

Ovelia turned the handle of the door, pushing it open, and we entered a room much smaller than the first. There were thousands of dead iguanas stacked in crates. The stench from the entrails was revolting. I felt my stomach heave, having to hold my hand over my mouth and breath deeply to keep from throwing up all over Ovelia.

We walked to the far end of the room. A number of men with very sharp knives were working wordlessly, cutting the entrails from iguana that had been sliced in half like filleted fish and with a further hand motion the guts were removed from the skin and swept into large buckets. "Where do you get all these iguana?" I had been facetious last night when I asked if Blackmore had enough room in his containers for all the skins, but now I meant it. It looked to me that there were enough skins here to make shoes for every man, woman and child in Europe.

Ovelia saw my revulsion. "We pay the locals to catch them. So much per skin."

"Are they a nuisance or dangerous or anything like that? Do the locals want to get rid of them?"

"No. It's just that with the refinery shutting down, jobs are scarce. People need the money."

"Oh." It was disgusting that Carlo would take advantage of these economic conditions to satisfy his own desires. The whole thing was creepy. I felt myself about to heave again.

Ovelia saw me put my hand to my stomach. "Are you okay? We don't have to stay. I know it's shocking to see this." Ovelia's cocoa skin had turned as pale as I was sure mine was.

"There are so many. If he's not careful he'll destroy every last iguana on Aruba."

"I know. I have brought this to Carlo's attention." She motioned me back toward the door through which we'd entered. "I've talked to him about using cow skins, but he is so excited about his new technique which requires a reptile's skin, he's adamant. There's nothing I can do."

I liked Ovelia more already.

"Come, Miss Howard, I will take you to my house. It is only a few blocks from here, just the other side of town. You look like you could use a drink."

"No. But thanks. I'll be okay. I'll just walk back to Carlo's."

"Are you sure? It is no problem for me to take you back."

"I need the walk." It was my turn to put my hand on her arm. "Really, I want to walk back. I need to clear my head."

I wandered the palm-lined streets of Oranjestad, the beauty I'd seen yesterday marred. I wondered what it would have looked like in the sixteenth century when the Dutch were a great seagoing power, imagined the sounds and smells of horse-drawn carriages instead of the line of exhaust-spewing automobiles made in Brazil that now clogged the streets. It occurred to me each technological "improvement" left in its wake a new menace to clean, a new problem to solve. *Instead of horse dung the air is infested with the heavy metals added to gasoline to make cars go faster, quicker, smoother.*

Where the hell are we going in such a hurry? Breeding five billion of us, that's where, each person is trying his damnedest to get ahead, have more stuff than the next guy. Humans are a greedy lot. I passed faces peering into shop windows. Faces carrying shopping bags full of new, coveted items. Faces leaving cafes and bars, stuffed with too much food and drink. Faces, faces, faces. The faces of people unwilling to critique their own behavior. At that moment I felt contempt for everything about the "civilized" world.

It's our decayed moral environment, I decided. We're de-moralized. We no longer know the difference between good and bad? The internal combustion engine has replaced our dependence on animal labor, but our desire for the latest fashions is destroying animals in the wild. With despair, I knew I was one of the "we."

With the acrid smell of the guts in Carlo's workshop still burning in my nostrils, I walked east, out of town. When I got to the white sand beach that led to Carlo's villa I took off the "passion red" Minellis and rubbed my fingers on the rough surface of the iguana skin. My body was drained of energy.

I thought about the iguana that had shared my lunch. It was obviously a sentient being, as the Buddhists say, definitely capable of figuring out what it wanted, planning a strategy and executing it with precision and cunning. It had forethought and passion. I couldn't believe unfeeling instinct was the only thing behind its behavior.

I walked in the shallow water, feeling a deep remorse for all animals that suffer ill treatment from humans. I remembered documentaries I'd seen on television about dogs that were beaten and abandoned. I'd read the economic history of civilizations that in their thirst for material advantage, worked their animals to death.

Shame clung to me like the smell of spoiling flesh, shame for the pride I'd taken in the red shoes, shame for the importance I had placed in my appearance. "Habit stupefies our senses," Montaigne had said.

I let the shoes fall into the foaming lace of the surf, watched the red leather soak up the salt water, and turn darker and darker as they bobbed about on the surface. Slowly, wave after wave moved the shoes farther from the shore. When I could see them no more I walked the mile or so to Carlo's villa not noticing the hot sun sear into my skin.

In front of the house, I waded into the breaking surf, until my body was submerged, my dress riding up as the water pushed its way between the fabric and my skin. I ducked under the next swell, pulling the dress over my head and stood naked, legs astride as the cleansing salt water rolled over me. But nothing, absolutely nothing could clear from my mind the picture of those hundreds of dead iguana being laboriously skinned. And all so women like me could wear sexy shoes and be feted by men like Carlo Minelli and Charles Blackmore who made money catering to our desires and weaknesses. Our insecurities. We'll buy anything to feel good, be more self-confident. It was sickening.

I walked out of the water, holding my dress in my hand, contemplating what I should do. The sun had just dropped below the horizon, leaving a soft glow completely out of synch with how I was still feeling. I looked up and Carlo and Blackmore were standing on the veranda watching me, wide-eyed. In my angst, I had forgotten they would be there.

I held my dress in front of me. "What are you staring at?" I didn't care I was naked. Lots of men have seen my body, but right now, they were intruding on my private feelings. The best defense is an offence, as my dad used to say. "I was at your disgusting plant today, Carlo. Slaughtering all those creatures to make a new fashion statement. It's an obscene way to get rich."

Blackmore grinned, but Carlo's face reddened, his eyes little slits.

"May I remind you, Miss Howard, you accepted a large amount of money for your part in this. And I believe my household has been pampering you in a manner you seem to enjoy."

"You're right, Carlo. That's why I quit. You'll get all your money back. All your murderous gain. So much for your angels. You're a butcher."

His face became even redder. But rather than facing Carlo directly I turned on Blackmore. "I've had a theory for a long time that nobody gets as rich as you two in one lifetime if they haven't done a lot of really bad stuff."

Before either of them could comment, I pushed my way past them, struggling to cover my butt with the dress and disappeared up the stairs, leaving wet sandy footprints on the pristine wooden floor.

I ran through the shower to get the salt off my skin and dressed hurriedly in jeans and a T-shirt and those ridiculously high heels I'd bought in Monaco. "Fuck, fuck, fuck." I took the credit card, money and return airline ticket Carlo had given me, out of my purse, and threw them on the bed. I tossed my things into my suitcases then yanked them out of the room, down to the veranda and out to the street.

The only other person I knew on Aruba was Ovelia. *We seemed to hit it off today. I have to hope she'll help me. She said her house was on the other side of town. A couple of miles from here. I can look her number up in a phone book when I reach a café or a laundromat.*

There were not many street lamps on this part of the road. The darkness closed in, dislocated shapes became threatening and sinister.

My pulse quickened. I wondered just how dangerous it was in Aruba at night. *That's easy, Pru. It's always dangerous where there are poor people.* Aruba has its share of disadvantaged. I could be raped or murdered.

For some unknown reason I remembered a conversation I'd once had with a girl who was hitchhiking around the world by herself. She carried a large backpack with bits of her stuff hanging on the outside.

"Where do you keep your credit card?" I'd asked her.

"In my shoe," she'd answered. "They never take off your shoes when they rape you." *Now that's a lovely thought when you're out here... alone.*

A car slowed down beside me. *Don't look. Just keep walking.* The wind was howling, but I could hear the driver roll down the passenger window. A male voice said something I couldn't make out.

My heart raced. *This could be it, Pru. You are about to find out if that girl was telling the truth.*

The car pulled in behind me and stopped. I dropped my bags and began to run. *What an absurd way to die.*

A hand reached out and grabbed my arm.

I turned to knee the guy.

He said my name.

I looked up into the face of Charles Blackmore. "You scared me, you idiot. What were you thinking?" The fear was gone but my anger about the dead iguana returned.

"Better me than all sorts of others. It's not safe. Please, get in the car."

I shook his hand loose. "I don't need your help."

He stepped back a pace, and started to chuckle. "I think you do. After we heard the door slam, the maid found the money, credit card, and airline ticket on the bed. Carlo told me you're broke. It seems to me you're in a strange country with no way to get home, wearing very high heels... too high for a walk into town. If you make it you'll be crippled for life. And remember, I'm Canadian. I don't leave women stranded by the side of the road." He looked at me quizzically. "Where were you going, anyway?"

It was my turn to laugh. I could see how nutty this must have looked to him. I was standing on principle, prepared to get myself killed or raped or at the very least, robbed for the sake of a small reptile I wasn't even sure he knew anything about.

"To Ovelia's."

Blackmore opened the car door for me then retrieved the bags I'd left beside the road.

"We'll have to stop somewhere and look up her address. She said she lives in town."

"I know where she lives. Ovelia and I are old friends."

I hadn't much time to contemplate the meaning of "old friends" before we were parked in front of her house, a small wooden structure painted a sunny yellow with turquoise trim. It was fenced with pickets the same yellow. Blackmore pushed the gate open and we walked to the covered porch bordered with a grouping of small cacti.

"She's out. Her jeep's not here." Blackmore noted.

"She told me she had to take her kids to something at school. It's okay. I'll just sit and wait." I moved to the porch swing, its white peeling paint revealed natural rattan underneath. Blackmore followed me up the wooden steps and sat down beside me. Our shoulders touched and a current of energy flowed between us making me suddenly warm.

"The wind isn't as brisk here in town," he said.

He was right. The air was still and rather humid. It must have showered briefly, earlier. Truthfully, the constant wind was getting on my nerves and with the upset over the iguana I was in no mood to make small talk with him or anyone else, but I had to say something. "I guess that's why the town was built here." My voice sounded stilted, uncomfortable. Damn, any other time and this would be the perfect setting to set my hooks into a guy like this. He's closer to my age than Carlo. Probably about thirty-seven or eight and Canadian. There'd be no cultural differences between us. What lousy timing.

"Yes, there's a wind shadow created by the mountain up behind us." Blackmore said.

"Ovelia won't be late. She has her kids with her. You don't have to keep me company. Really, I'll be fine."

"Sorry, I can't be a true knight saving a damsel in distress until she's turned over to the proper authorities. We can spend the time by you telling me all about yourself."

I wasn't buying, even though a small voice in my head kept saying that his coming to rescue me was kind of sweet. "You can stay if you want but I don't have to talk to you or be nice. You saved me because you have some fetish about being a knight errant. I didn't ask for your help."

"Ah, but you admit I did save you."

I chuckled again.

"You know, we could go somewhere and get a drink. Dinner if you want...come back later when she's sure to be home."

"No thanks." As much as I wanted a drink, I couldn't consort with the enemy. "Look, have you ever been to Carlo's workshop?"

"No."

"You should some time. See what he does to make money."

We sat in silence for some time watching the boats in the marina at the bottom of Ovelia's street. The reflection from mast lights and salon windows danced across the water. I looked at him through the corner of my eye. His face had character, but he was stiff, careful even though he had tried to make me laugh. There was something he was hiding, or hiding from. *I wonder what it is he doesn't want people to know about him?*

Blackmore turned to me and smiled. "Okay. I'll talk. You can just sit and listen or daydream or whatever you want."

Now that's really annoying. He's being so nice. But I guess it beats sitting here alone with my own discomfited thoughts.

"I told you I knew Ovelia's father. He was a good, sound governor. Conscientious. Never took graft or did anything to further his own fortune."

I said nothing but felt a sense of relief. *That's why he and Ovelia are old friends.*

"He died a few years ago. About the time Ovelia's husband ran off. She bought this house with her inheritance. You can see by the size of it, he didn't leave her a lot of money."

"What about her mother?" In spite of what I'd said, I was becoming interested.

"She was killed in a hit and run accident when Ovelia was nine. I don't think Ovelia or her father ever got over it. She's an only child, her father's pet. With just the two of them after the accident, they became very close. She was his right hand man at work. Actually, she could run this island. She has a real head for business and she cares deeply about Aruba."

"Why isn't she doing that, then, instead of working for Carlo?" I became increasingly aware of the earthy, musty scent emanating from Blackmore, so I stood up and moved to lean against the porch railing, to try to eliminate my increasing desire.

"When Ovelia became a teenager, in the early seventies, she went through a bit of a wild streak...started to identify with the reggae music coming out of Jamaica. Protest stuff. But she didn't have anything to protest. Her maternal grandparents had fled from Jamaica with their young kids to what they hoped would be a better life on Aruba. And it was. Ovelia's mother married Adolph Steinmetz and lived a nice life as the governor's wife.

"But you know teenagers. Bob Marley was Ovelia's hero. All the talk about freedom. She fell in love with Aston, who wore dreadlocks and talked about repatriating blacks like himself back to Ethiopia so they could be in the bosom of the Rastafarian religion."

I regretted standing. My feet were killing me. *Why did Carlo have to use the iguana skins? If they were cowhide I could still be working for him and Charles and I could be having this conversation over a glass of wine.*

Blackmore said, "They got married and Ovelia started to have babies. Aston was a carpenter, a very good one. But he never gave up his dream. He was saving money for tickets to Africa, but what he didn't realize was Ovelia had outgrown it all. When the time came, she wouldn't go. She preferred to raise her boys here. So they split. Occasionally she gets a letter from him. Bits of money. But he's taken another wife and has more kids."

"That's quite a story," I said. "Not many women would be able to get through all that."

"She's tough. But it's easier now that she works for Carlo. As you know, he's very generous with his employees."

That might explain why Ovelia seemed so uncomfortable at the warehouse. She likes Carlo and the money, but is conflicted about the slaughter. *It's easy for me to be righteous. I don't have to raise three kids on my own.*

Ovelia's jeep pulled up to the curb and her three boys piled out. "What is it? Has something happened to Carlo?"

Interesting her first thought would be Carlo's well being. She must be in love. "No. Carlo's fine. It's me. I need to talk to you. Mr. Blackmore kindly drove me here, but..." I looked at Blackmore. "He was just leaving."

Ovelia looked from me to Charles, a quizzical look on her face. "Can't you come in for a drink, Charles? The kids haven't seen you for a long time." She dropped her keys into the large handbag she was carrying and came forward to give Blackmore a kiss on the cheek.

"I can't, sorry." He knelt down and let the boys give him a hug. "I'll come by before I leave, though."

He drove off, and I followed Ovelia into the house. Bookcases lined the walls. Two chintz-covered chairs with long thick fringe below the seat, sat between a table with a large lamp and a bookmarked book, Aldous Huxley's modern classic, *Point Counterpoint. Ovelia's not just another pretty face.*

"I'm sorry to trouble you this late. With the boys and all, but I need to talk to you."

The kids ran through an arched doorway into the kitchen. “I have to get them something to eat before bed. Then I’ll want a glass of wine. I was worried about you and it’s been a long day.”

I followed Ovelia to the rear of the house. She took a slab of cheese from the fridge and sliced it onto dark bread. The boy’s rambunctious behavior stopped as they became conscious of a stranger amongst them. She introduced Adam, Zack, and Robert to me and they each politely shook my hand. Then the ate the snack and drank the milk Ovelia poured into small glasses.

The kitchen table was beautifully crafted, round, and made of pine, white-washed so the grain showed through. Four tub chairs woven from palm fronds and stained deep red, sat around it. I wondered if her husband, Aston, had made the table.

I watched as she got her boys into bed. The love between them was palpable, like a textured fabric that I felt I could reach out and touch. Would I ever want this? *Perhaps it’s best left to the pure of heart.*

When they were at last asleep, she poured us a glass of wine in her living room and I could see her shoulders relax. “What is it you need to talk about?”

“I was so shocked about the iguana, I quit my job.” I gulped my wine and told her about the episode on the beach, which in the re-telling seemed hilarious to me. “I’m so frigging mad at Carlo, I’ve given back the airline ticket, the credit card, and the money he advanced me. Now I’m destitute and probably can’t work here without some kind of visa or landed immigrant status or something.” I drained the glass of wine and Ovelia had enough sense to re-fill it.

"I don't have any influence with the government now my father's gone, if that's what you're thinking?"

"No, that's not it. I took the job with Carlo because it meant I would have enough cash to support myself back in Europe while I finish writing my novel."

"Have you almost completed it?"

"Not exactly. My agent loves what I've sent him. He's found a publisher that's interested, but I can't get the antagonist to jell." I drained my glass. "As if I don't know anything about disreputable men."

She gave me a droll look. And we burst out laughing, both thinking about Carlo, I was sure. "You have an agent. That's impressive. Are you a famous author I just haven't heard about, down here in Aruba?"

"I wish. My mother went to school with a literary agent named Sid Cosgrow. He's been mentoring me for years and managed to get my first efforts published. I get regular royalty cheques, but it's not big money. Truthfully, I haven't been as prudent as my name would suggest. But another payment is due in a couple of weeks. If the past trends continue there should be enough there to get me a ticket back to Canada where I can probably sponge off my dad for a while. I feel I'm on to something with this book. Other than this character Bentley, as I told you. All I need is some quiet time to concentrate."

"Strengthening one character doesn't sound like it would take very long."

"It shouldn't."

She bit into the cheese she held in her slender fingers. "You can stay here as long as you need to."

"How did you know what I was going to ask?" *As long as I needed. That was generous.* I wouldn't have offered that to a woman I'd just met. It couldn't be cheap to run a house with three growing boys. I was used to taking the largesse of men with means, but could I accept the generosity of a mother with three children. This was a low point, even for me.

She shrugged. "Call it woman's intuition, Prudence. Besides, I'll enjoy the adult company. It gets overwhelming sometimes. I don't have a guest room, though. You'll have to sleep on the sofa bed here in the living room."

Knowing she would benefit from the arrangement helped relieve my guilt but I added, "If you'll let me do the cooking and cleaning, and if you call me Pru, like my other friends, I'll accept." I looked at the wine and cheese she had provided. "And I'll keep a tab of what I cost you. One more thing. I'm prone to nightmares. Sometimes I scream out loud, so if I do, you might have to come out here and wake me up. I don't want to scare your boys."

"Not to worry. We're all heavy sleepers. We probably won't even hear you."

Ovelia paused, lost in thought. I studied her groomed appearance, her hair pulled tightly back from her face emphasizing its oval curve. Her lips were parted displaying a row of perfect, very white teeth. She turned thickly lashed eyes towards me.

Ovelia said, "I'm disturbed by what's happening, as well. I care about the iguana even though they're not terribly beautiful. You know. All the scales and long toe-like claws. Not exactly cuddly looking, like a cat."

"I know what you mean. For me, I just appreciate any creature that lives in the wild under the laws nature has dictated. And doing it successfully unless man, or in our case, a specific man comes along and puts hundreds of them to death." I looked up and Ovelia had gone white under her tan skin. I might have just put my foot in it.

"Are you in a relationship with Carlo?" I asked.

She seemed reluctant to answer.

"Look, it doesn't matter. I'm not sleeping with him."

A look of shock passed over her face. "I thought you were."

"You must be some kind of a saint. You've been very nice to me from the moment I arrived, considering you thought I was your rival."

Ovelia topped up our wine and passed me the plate of cheese and crackers.

"I'm very attracted to Carlo. But, to him I'm just another employee. I'm sure he has his pick of attractive models in Milan. I can't compete with all that beauty. So, rather than being a saint, as you put it, I've accepted the fact he's not interested in me."

"I can't say how Carlo feels. I've never talked to him about you, but I wouldn't give up hope. You're as good looking as any model I've ever seen. I'm jealous of you just as a matter of principle."

Now that the tension of a potential rivalry was dissipated, warmth was developing between us. What really impressed me was she told the truth. If she'd lied, I would have realized it and there would always have been this "thing" between us. But she hadn't.

The next day, after we saw the boys off to school and Ovelia left for work, I sat at the kitchen table overlooking a neat garden enclosed by a high stone wall covered with espaliered purple bougainvillea. Lush pink impatiens grew under an enormous palm, its leafy shade, like Matisse cutouts.

I was struggling with a piece of dialogue spoken by Bentley Tyler when I heard the front door open.

"That was a short day, Ovelia. You've only been at work for an hour."

"I quit."

"What? Why?"

"You showed me how to be brave."

"Me?" *That was a good one. It was Ovelia who'd saved me.* "But, what will you do? You have the boys." *Now, I don't mind being an example of how women can make their way in the world, but I draw the line at mothers with small children. My life style is for the single and foolhardy.*

"I have a plan. Something I've been thinking about for some time. You showed me you have to trust yourself."

I poured her a coffee. If I talked some sense into her, maybe she could get her job back. But it might not be easy; I could see she was glowing with inner joy. *She has the ability to come up against something ugly and not let it touch her. She stays pure, while I, I've become cynical, the legacy of a disillusioned idealist.*

She saw the look of panic on my face. "Now, don't start to worry, Prudence...I mean, Pru. I know what I'm doing. I'm going to start my own shoe factory. I have some ideas. Ideas Carlo didn't like."

"A shoe factory. That'll cost a whack of dough."

Ovelia put her coffee mug on the table and looked out the window. "When my father died, I inherited a small sum of money. Not much is left after buying this house, but it's enough to get my idea started."

She turned to me. "My father wanted me to make an independent life for the boys and myself." She took a deep breath and brushed away a tear. "Sorry, I still get upset when I think of him."

"It's okay. I can only guess what it's like to lose your dad."

"With my legacy as a down-payment, all I need to do is convince the bank my idea is sound and I can keep food on the table while I get the business going. Don't look so doubtful, Pru. Last night I couldn't sleep, so I sat down with paper and pencil and worked out a plan. I'm good with figures. My father taught me everything he knew about running this island. A small business is a piece of cake."

I remembered Charles Blackmore had said she was capable of being governor and decided to trust his judgment. "Okay...but, if I've truly been the inspiration for this mad idea, I don't want anything to go wrong. I couldn't live with myself."

"I've wanted to do this for some time. I was as disgusted as you were by the slaughter of the iguana. It's not just the killing of a wild animal that bothers me. The Green Iguana is unique to Aruba. Truth be told, my father wouldn't have wanted me involved in Carlo's business." Ovelia's voice cracked with emotion. "I let my feelings for him get in the way of doing the right thing. You showed me I should stand up for my principles. Even if it will break my heart."

It's such a drag to be reminded about reality. I've always liked living in my imagination.

Ovelia brought me from my thoughts. "It's kind of like

I'm a trolley bus, you know the kind that run by attaching a long pole to an electrical line. Sometimes those poles flip off the line and the bus stops. Have you seen the drivers get out of the trolley and try to reattach the connection? He tries one side, then the other, with the pole flopping uselessly until suddenly he gets it attached, returns to the drivers seat and the trolley takes off. That's what it feels like to me. That I've just become attached to my energy source."

"Wow, I get it."

"Pru, enough of me. I've done it, so that's that," Ovelia said, displaying her Dutch stoicism. "Tell me about the book. All I know is one of the characters is giving you problems, but I don't even know the plot."

"It's about a woman, Stella, who was born to English parents on their farm in Zimbabwe. The family returned to Britain after Robert Mugabe became president. Stella goes back for a vacation a few years later. When she's older. She's horrified to learn the black rhino are facing extinction. Being brutally killed. Their horns ground down and used as aphrodisiacs or sold for talismans."

"What kind of talismans?"

"In Yemen they're prized as dagger handles and in the Orient the keratin which is a fibrous protein found in hair is considered an aphrodisiac worth about half its weight in gold."

"That's why your character, Bentley Tyler, is willing to traffic in the horns. Right?"

"I have no problem with people eating meat, I eat it myself. As long as the animals are looked after. Raised properly. But animals in the wild. It makes me crazy. I was on safari once in Zimbabwe. I saw..." The memory was so intense, a shiver went through me. "One morning our guide asked if we wanted to track a lion that was hunting in the area. We set off in an open jeep. After about half an hour we stopped in an area of open savanna. We could hear the lion in the distance calling. The guide told us that meant the animal had already eaten and we were unlikely to find him. But he thought we might spot some rhino. At the edge of a scrub forest, we did. A dead one. The jackals were already at work ripping the flesh away. But the guide scared them off with his gun. We got out of the jeep and approached the huge carcass."

"It's a three year old," the guide said. "Fully grown."

"There was blood where the jackals had started to rip through the thick brown skin. Actually plate-like folds. What we think dinosaur skin would be like. Then I saw that its horn had been gouged off its face. By poachers. It looked pathetic maimed like that. We stood in silence and I was crying. I clutched my fists so tightly I drew blood."

"'The people are hungry,'" the guide had said, "'but if these poachers are caught doing this, they're in real trouble.' He explained that's why they just leave the meat. You see, when Mugabe gave the land back to the people, the tribes, an acre or two each, all their relatives left the cities and just showed up. Sometimes hundreds of them. The land can't provide enough. Farming isn't efficient anymore. Honestly, Ovelia, if one of those poachers had appeared I would have killed *him*. That beautiful, sentient being slaughtered for its horn. I touched it. It was still warm. Then I saw it had long curly eyelashes."

"Really?"

"Yes. Beautiful long eyelashes."

Ovelia reached over and put her hand on my arm, calming me. I took a sip of my now tepid coffee. "Anyway, that's why I wanted to write this book. Maybe if people know this is happening, someone will do something to stop the poaching."

"That's why you were so upset about the iguana, isn't it?'

"Yes. There is a parallel. In my novel, Stella's angry, of course, and in her attempt to put a stop to the useless killing, she uncovers all sorts of other illegal activities and is nearly killed herself while trying to help the authorities round up the mob responsible."

"That sounds like a real page turner. It'll sell."

I read a bit to her. "But I just can't get the antagonist right. Bentley Tyler's too much of a caricature of the bad guy. So one-dimensional." I dropped the pages onto the table. "I'm doomed. My publisher won't want this dreck."

"Well, seems to me the story would be more interesting if your heroine falls for this Bentley before she realizes he's a crook. You'd have to make him a more complex, engaging guy, in order for that to be believable," Ovelia stated in her quiet way.

Out of the mouths of the mothers of babes. Why hadn't I thought of that?

So, while Ovelia sat at one end of the kitchen table writing a business plan, I began to re-write Bentley Tyler, loosely modeled after Charles Blackmore, a man I could become passionate about...a man with style, charisma, and money. But he was also a ruthless, sophisticated arms dealer who trafficked in illegal ivory and black rhino horns. Bentley Tyler resorted to murder to protect his empire.

As I wrote, I realized that the container-shipping business was the perfect front for all sorts of illegal trade. What Tyler/Blackmore had begun as a legitimate, useful business, power and money had corrupted. It fit perfectly with my thesis that it was impossible to make a stupendous fortune in one lifetime without resorting to illegal or nasty dealings. The story just flowed. Ovelia and I fell easily into a simple routine. Each day we got the boys ready for school before she headed to her new factory. I cleaned the kitchen then sat at the table and wrote. Each night after the boys were in bed I read my pages to Ovelia who praised the bits she liked and gave useful comments when she felt the writing was lacking.

One night we sat as a rain shower broke with violence, thundering on the roof so we were shouting at each other. "You've really nailed this guy, Pru." Then just as suddenly, the clouds parted and the last brilliant rays of the sun shone. "I've known Charles a long time. But you've made Bentley so believable I'm beginning to wonder if Charles could be doing just what you've described."

I looked up from the manuscript. "I do seem to have a great imagination for wickedness. I doubt Charles' mind would even go there. He seems to be on the up and up."

After I made the final corrections, I sent the opening chapters of the revised manuscript to Sid and then all there was to do was wait. But I woke in the middle of the night and thought about what Ovelia had said. Bentley Tyler's activities would be so easy for a man with a shipping-container business. And I had made Bentley Tyler into a completely believable conman. After all, charisma is a requirement for successful manipulators.

Carlo Minelli's Villa

Aruba

"Ah, my friend," Carlo began. "I am sorry you had to witness that upsetting turn of events. I think Miss Prudence Howard is overly sensitive to the plight of animals. These creatures were placed here by God to supply man with his needs, no?"

Blackmore was now sitting at the dining table where Prudence Howard's place setting had been removed. An hour before, Carlo had agreed that no woman, not even one who enraged him, should walk alone at night on the road into town. While waiting for Blackmore's return he'd been listening to Vivaldi on the stereo, a usually uplifting experience, but his expression was still as pained as the darkness that stared in at them.

Blackmore's mouth was full of lettuce greens and he took the opportunity to consider his response. His leanings were more with Prudence Howard, but he didn't want to aggravate his host. "Women do have a tendency to anthropomorphize animals. My mother treated our cats as if they were my siblings. But you must agree, Carlo, we humans intrude on nature for our own benefit." Blackmore stopped, another leaf of lettuce aloft on his fork. "What did she mean about your angels, Carlo? If you don't mind my asking."

Carlo rubbed his hand over his balding head. "My business...I do it to glorify the memory of my first and only love. My Angelita.

"Charles, I think we share the passion of doing things well. It is an understanding beyond business. If you have the patience, I will tell you what I have told no one in forty years."

Blackmore nodded his assent, honoured the Italian was willing to share something so personal.

The salad plates were removed and Carlo signaled to the steward for more wine to be poured. "I have told you, I believe, how I learned to make shoes in Naples and then my fortuitous meeting with the glove maker who taught me how to work with soft leathers. But now, about my angels.

"You see...I don't remember a time when I couldn't draw. 'A gift from God,' my mother told me, 'like Michelangelo.' I drew angels for her from my imagination. It was the greatest gift I could give her."

Blackmore leaned back into the upholstered dining chair and lifted his glass of wine to the candlelight. As he took a sip he thought of his mother, back in Edmonton. She was a stiff, shy woman who always did her husband's bidding. She had neither inspired Charles nor was she a person from whom to flee. She had loved him, that was all.

Carlo said, "But these drawings were only to prepare me for meeting my Angelita after I moved to Amalfi."

Sautéed veal shanks were placed before the two men. Blackmore inhaled the pungent spicy fragrance then cut into the tender meat.

Carlo continued, "I hoped to find a job in a hotel. You see, I yet had no idea how to turn my newfound skill as a shoemaker into a commercial success.

"There still is a hotel that sits on the sand on the west side of town, just as the road begins to ascend. It catered to small groups of tourists who took their meals in the hotel restaurant. They needed help in the kitchen."

"The Hotel La Busola?"

"Yes, you know it?"

"I've stayed there many times."

"The maitre d', who also did the hiring, gave me directions to the home of an elderly woman, Senora Ponti, who he was sure would give me a room...if I promised not to cause trouble. Her home was almost at the end of the street that runs toward the mountain. You recall the pedestrian street, no? Near the end, a small path leads up the mountain to another village. Have you walked on that ancient terraced land? They grow the large Amalfi lemons for which the region is famous."

"Delicious. Almost as big as an orange."

"Yes, Yes. Well, Senora Ponti lived only a short distance above the town on a small patch of earth where she grew vegetables and herbs for her brother's restaurant. I still remember the sweet scent of basil as I walked through the wooden gate. It reminded me of my mother's garden.

"The aromas inside were even more enticing. Senora Ponti told me she was cooking a leg of lamb she'd marinated in lemon juice and the whey from buttermilk before roasting it in more lemon and garlic. She must have seen the hunger in my eyes because after she had agreed to rent the room to me, she invited me to share her dinner."

The steward poured more wine and Carlo relinquished his salad, largely uneaten. But he took a large gulp of wine. "One night not long after I had arrived, Senora Ponti told me her grand niece was to be married and the two families were getting together at her brother's restaurant for an informal celebration of the forthcoming union. 'You're such a good boy, Carlo, and so far from home. You must come,' she had said. Truth be told, I grieved the loss of my family and I missed Rosa, the girlfriend I'd had in Sicily, the one I made the red shoes for, if you remember. I agreed to go, telling myself Senora Ponti would need my arm to help her get to the party and back at night."

"The small restaurant was full of people when we arrived. It was an intimate place with low ceilings and thick plastered walls painted the color of the Amalfi sun. Rust and yellow checked cloths covered each table which also held an empty Chianti bottle with its rush covered base holding a lit candle. The family was drinking the local wine from earthen jugs, the room resounding with conversations and laughter.

"Senora Ponti introduced me to so many of her relatives that my head was swimming like the noodles in my minestrone soup. I met the bride to be, but it was her younger sister, Angelita that I could not take my eyes from. She glowed with an inner radiance, like pure burnished gold. I was instantly in love. I couldn't stop staring at her delicate almond shaped face. She was warm, gracious, and well loved by everyone.

"Senora Ponti saw that I was love-struck. 'She is well-named, no, Carlo?'

"In spite of all the beautiful angels I had imagined and drawn for my mother, none was as lovely as this girl. Divine was the only word I could think of to describe her. She was my Beatrice. I could, at last, understand Dante's motivation to reach his beloved.

"I learned that she was the lunch hostess at her father's restaurant so I began to take my mid-day meal there even though I could eat for free in the kitchen of the hotel. As was my way, I noticed her feet. They were as perfect as the rest of her. Not yet damaged like Rosa's from too many nights in high heels. Angelita wore the flat sandals of a girl. My desire was to see what she looked like in the shoes I had made for Rosa. I tossed and turned in bed that night, tormented by longing as I imagined her beautiful feet in the shoes. In the morning I wrapped them in a velvet cloth, tying my package with a large golden ribbon. At the end of my shift, I hurried to the restaurant.

"When Angelita had seated the lunch guests, she sat with me as had become her custom. Awkwardly, I shoved the package at her. She blushed, the most beautiful shade of pink. I have tried unsuccessfully to mix that color with pigment, but, alas, with no success. It is the color of angels.

"She put them on and held out her feet, examining my work from every angle. Then, she stood. In that moment I saw the change in her. My shoes transformed her into a woman. I thought my heart would stop."

"Is that when you got the idea to start your atelier?"

"No, I still had no idea that I could do that. But, I soon learned that she returned my affection and we married. We were blissfully happy. For a year. But then the war intervened. I was made to serve in Mussolini's army."

"The war. I've never thought of you as a soldier."

"The casualties started mounting. Angelita went to Rome as a volunteer nurse. There were so many deaths..." Carlo ran his hand over his balding head again. "Such painful memories..."

"You lost many of your friends, I guess."

"Of course, but it was Angelita. After our surrender to the Allies and our combined armies began to chase the Nazi's out or Italy..." Carlo paused and took in a tortured breath. He cradled his head in his hands and Blackmore could see he was shaking. "She was raped and beaten by a retreating German soldier."

"Oh, my god." Blackmore felt like he had just been hit in the pit of the stomach.

Carlo took another large gulp of wine and motioned for more to be poured. "I had no idea at the time that it had happened. They sent her back to Amalfi to recover. But they didn't know she was pregnant.

"One day after the restaurant closed for the afternoon, she walked the narrow winding path up behind Signora Ponti's cottage to the small village that perches on the promontory above Amalfi. Once at the top she sat on the terrace of the small bistro that overlooks the water hundreds of feet below. The owner reported she ordered a glass of freshly squeezed lemonade and drank it never taking her eyes off the ocean below.

"Then..." Carlo's eyes brimmed with tears. "She walked to the edge of the terrace and took off her shoes. Then she unclasped her hair so that it flowed in the breeze, like the angel I knew her to be. She stepped off the terrace to her death."

Blackmore was stunned. No wonder Carlo had never remarried. How could he after such a catastrophe? Blackmore reached over and put his hand on the Italian's arm.

"When I finally returned and learned what happened. She left a note for me. I was, as you can imagine, in agony.

Nothing I felt for her was changed by that hideous incident. I would have loved the child. I felt overwhelming guilt that I had not loved her well enough for her to trust me. I had to leave. Everything reminded me of her. Not that I wouldn't think of her every day, but I couldn't bear the way they all looked at me, not with pity, but with shared love.

"I carefully wrapped the shoes and headed north. Eventually I found myself back in Milan. For weeks I wandered the streets with my sacred package in my arms.

"After a while, the pain shifted. It never left, just moved aside far enough for me to notice when I was hungry or thirsty, or tired. I began again to see all the cramped and sore feet of women who walked past me in the street. Then it was as if my Angelita came to me. Spoke to me, like a whispered message from God, telling me what I should do.

"I rented a small workshop. I perfected my designs and soon wealthy women sought out my atelier to buy Minelli shoes. It is my ongoing tribute to Angelita that each woman feels as my angel did when she put the shoes on her feet."

For a moment there was just the sound from the stereo of the violins playing a sweet concerto. Blackmore drained the last of his wine thinking how inappropriate the music was to this scene. "How unbelievably tragic. Few men have suffered such a loss, Carlo."

Although Carlo thought he could trust this Canadian, he felt open, vulnerable, something he had not felt in a long time. He drank the last of his wine then stood up. "Now if you don't mind, Charles, I'm tired."

Charles Blackmore

Aruban Shores Hotel

Blackmore returned to his hotel room and crawled into the starched white sheets of the king size bed, alone. The wind had picked up and he could hear the palms being lashed about. Each time he looked at the numbers on the bedside clock only another fifteen minutes had passed, thoughts tumbling about in his mind.

He was sure that he had the potential to fall deeply in love. What kept him awake was the question: why had he never let himself feel love for someone, the way Carlo had for Angelita? Even if love ended in unbelievable sadness and loss, surely such an intense experience would justify the pain?

Then he thought about his accomplishments, about Blackmore Shipping, the last fifteen years of hard, albeit, interesting work. Building the company had absorbed all his time and energy. Because he lived alone he could concentrate fully on the business. If he'd had a wife or a long-term lover, he would have had to consider her needs.

He reached over and turned on the light, but the dark night pushing in on the white walls of the room made him feel even lonelier. He switched it off and rolled over. The jumbled thoughts kept coming.

As his business expanded, he had become part of the world of commerce and industry. It gave his life meaning. And, he had his art. He thought of the painting he left unfinished in London, one in a series of sensuous abstracts that gave him so much pleasure. He would be home soon and relished the thought of losing himself in the voluptuousness of the oils, the feeling of filling a brush with rich, lustrous pigment and then dragging it slowly over the unprimed canvas.

His passion to experience other cultures had never left him. And being his own boss meant he lived as if he were on assignment for *National Geographic* except he chose the assignments. Somehow he had a sense for the next great tourist destination that was currently off the beaten path. He'd get his fill of its rustic, traditional ambiance and then he was happy to transport all the amenities the softer travelers required: the pipes for hot and cold running water, clean sheets and mosquito nets. By facilitating the import and export of goods he had helped small economies grow.

His eyes opened at the thought that perhaps Prudence Howard could be right. Was he an unethical opportunist who, in his own small way, contributed to the destruction of the very places he loved? Was he simply a money-grubbing, unconscious fool?

He got up and walked into the living room, flicking on the satellite television. The voices of the actors in the old black and white re-run made it seem as if he were not alone. He poured himself a large scotch and added ice, hoping it would help him sleep. On the screen the actor Spencer Tracey scowled at another actor whose name Blackmore couldn't remember. He took a large gulp of the drink and felt it burn his throat.

He rationalized that someone else would have traded with those countries if he hadn't. But, instead of material success, what if he had transferred some of his passion for making money to a particular woman? Would he have been happier? Would the world have been a better place? He sighed. He was proud that he had more of most things than one man could expect. And, damn it, he'd worked hard for it.

He remembered the morning in 1968 when Pembroke had called him into his office for his first and as it turned out, fateful, assignment abroad.

Lord Pembroke had received a request from Adnan Bartok to insure his fishing fleet in Morocco, in a town on the west coast called Essaouira. Blackmore was to inspect their operation.

When the plane landed in Casablanca, Blackmore, who had been filled with images of the Humphrey Bogart movie he'd relished as a kid, watching it every time it came on TV, had jumped into a cab asking to be taken to the Café American, or Rick's Bar.

The driver just shook his head. "There is no such bar, Monsieur. You are thinking, perhaps of the movie?"

"Yes." Blackmore felt ridiculous. How could he have mistaken a movie for real life?

"There is a bar in the centre of town which boasts large posters of the famous actor, Humphrey Bogart. Would you like to go there?"

"No, thanks. Hotel Casablanca will be fine."

They drove through broad, treed streets, lined with white stucco buildings covered in layers of dust and grime. The city was definitely more dingy than he had anticipated.

He admonished himself. You're in a country with different customs, a different standard of living. Relax. See it for what it is, not some romantic notion you've conjured up in your head.

After giving himself this little lecture, Blackmore sat back in the cab and began to take in the sights with an eye for what was unique. The tall spire of a mosque, the first he'd ever seen, thrust upward in the distance. He ignored the faded grandeur and the garbage that floated along the curbs and sidewalks of the once- prosperous French protectorate. At the hotel he registered and then arranged transport to the town of Essaouira for early the next morning.

His hotel room was ill lit, and the view of the central courtyard was partly obscured by a large heating duct. The dark wooden furniture covered brown marble tiles, adding to the gloom of the place. His sense of apprehension grew. He was sure his friends in London would be put off by this place. Then he admonished himself again. He should enjoy what was different about this country.

The next morning Blackmore climbed into an ancient Mercedes diesel that coughed and sputtered as it pulled away from the curb. "Take me to the port before we leave town." He wanted to get an idea of the level of sophistication of the local shipping, so he could compare it with that in Essaouria.

It was a busy port. Lord Pembroke had told him the Moroccans exported large quantities of phosphates, cork, wheat and almonds. He was surprised to see how labor intensive the process of loading and unloading was. Large gangplanks extended from ship to shore. Men carried sacks of each item. There seemed to be no mechanization. It reminded him of a painting he'd seen by Monet at the Louvre in which the artist had depicted a barge being unloaded on the Seine. That picture was painted a hundred and fifty years ago. The Moroccan method provides lots of jobs, he thought, but it's terribly inefficient.

The highway to Essaouira was in excellent condition, a legacy of the French. The old car ground its way up and down rolling hills, passing small villages of earthen houses that rose out of the brown landscape. The barrenness was broken by herds of grazing sheep and the occasional overladen donkey. Blackmore felt for the stoic animals. Life was not easy here for beasts of burden.

As they neared the sea, the white walls and buildings of Essaouira shimmering in the blazing sun were shocking in contrast. As they drove closer Blackmore could see that Prussian blue tiles surrounded all the doors and windows of each building, matching the ocean beyond.

Towering above the town were the defensive walls of a fort with its stone parapet; the guidebook said it was a combination of Portuguese, French and Berber military architecture. After his meeting was over, Blackmore promised himself he'd investigate the old town.

The cab turned south, heading for the marina that was outside the walls of the town. Countless birds were rising and falling in waves, screeching their high-pitched call, a sure sign that fish boats were at hand. He dismissed the driver a few blocks from the docks so he could get a feel for the place.

The sun was directly overhead and it seared into his skin through his cotton shirt. Adjacent to the boat basin, fish were being grilled on braziers; tuna, sardines and other varieties he couldn't identify. A fisherman, with a rugged, weathered face and thick calloused fingers encrusted with grime from the hard life at sea, served Blackmore the fillets. He sat under an awning at one of the wooden tables provided. The fish was so fresh, like nothing he'd ever tasted, the savoury juices clinging to his chin.

After lunch he wandered up the street toward the town. He passed a two-storied wall with an enormous wooden door. It was open and Blackmore was curious. He walked across the street and looked inside. It was an ancient caravansary, a large courtyard open to the sky in the centre, with a tiled fountain sunk into the floor from which the animals could drink. An arcade ran around the enclosure and led to rooms where the men slept and ate after they had couched and unloaded their camels. The route connected the interior of Africa, Timbuktu and beyond, with the coast, trading salt, gold and other precious items. Blackmore felt a rush of excitement. This was the real thing, not some Disneyland imitation.

Out on the street he turned back toward the boat basin. In the proscribed place, he found Adnan Bartok, the fishing fleet owner, and a translator, and was taken on a tour of the boat-building operation. Adnan was in his fifties, Blackmore guessed; a slight, sinewy man with the same weathered fingers of a long time fisherman. But Adnan also had the intense eyes of a wary businessman.

The fishing boats were small by British standards, but meticulously built of wood according to long-held traditions whereby the planking that formed the sides of the boats was joined at the stem and stern. The boat hulls were mounted on large wooden stays that held them on dry dock where the work took place. Blackmore was impressed by the skill of the artisans at work.

Next Adnan took him to his small office on the dock. Records were kept in large hand-bound books. The Arabic script was impossible for Blackmore to decipher, but the numbers that they spent the rest of the meeting going over, looked in order; Lord Pembroke would insure Adnan's fleet.

"Mr. Blackmore, will you do me the honour of having your evening meal at my home. I live in the old city and I can show you some of the sights as we walk."

"I have made arrangements to meet my driver just after dark, which by the look of the light will be in about an hour."

"Don't worry about your man. I will send one of my boys to meet him and give him dinner. You can drive back to Casa later this evening."

Blackmore, Adnan and the translator were soon walking within the walls of the town. Along the narrow street Adnan stopped to show Blackmore the work of craftsmen who were sewing the traditional robes of the region, to which they applied intricate embroidery around the neck opening. Then they went into a bakery where it was explained to him that each morning the local housewives brought their leavened dough to be baked.

The narrow street soon opened onto a large square that was bustling with people. Braziers were set up here, too, but this time lamb was being grilled. Savoury smoke hung in the air. Many of the local men and women wore the long robes he had seen being embroidered. Someone close at hand jangled a tambourine. It was like nothing he had ever experienced, mesmerizing, exotic.

They walked up a flight of stairs and Blackmore found himself on the ramparts of the fort.

"These brass canon were placed here by the Portuguese in the 1500's," Adnan said.

Blackmore recalled from his high school history that the Portuguese had been the first to round the southern extent of Africa on their search for a sea route to the spice islands of the Far East and had established these defensive forts in order for the ships to take on stores.

Adnan turned into an alley and knocked at an unadorned wooden door identical to the others they had passed. It was opened and a servant bowed deeply. Blackmore followed Adnan into a courtyard around which was a balcony with doors leading off, he guessed, to the sleeping quarters. The courtyard was open to the night sky but trellised with reeds to protect it from the mid-day heat. Intricately patterned carpets and large plush cushions covered the floor. Potted plants in large glazed pots were placed about the room. Adnan took his place leaning into a group of cushions and told Blackmore to make himself comfortable.

"Bring us some tea, Mahmoud," Adnan commanded.

Soon another servant appeared carrying a large brass tray he placed on the low wooden table that stood before the men. Each was given a small bowl of washing water and a perfumed towel. Then another tray loaded with roasted chickens cut into large chunks was placed on the table.

"It is our custom to share food," Adnan said. "Please, help yourself."

Blackmore hesitated and Adnan repeated, "Go ahead, help yourself."

Realizing he was supposed to use his hands as no utensils were provided, Blackmore grabbed the leg of one of the chickens, the fat and olive oil sticking to his fingers. Unaccustomed spices stimulated his taste buds. He chewed, smiling his approval at Adnan who only then dug his fingers into the chicken and extracted the piece he wanted. The translator did the same.

Soon more trays appeared. One held a mound of couscous in the centre of which onions and raisins rested in a saffron sauce. Just as Blackmore felt he was full to bursting another tray appeared covered with a conical tagine lid. Inside was a lamb and almond stew flavoured with ginger and garlic, the aroma rising from the glistening sauce. There was flat bread for dipping. Finally came a tray of small date cakes that were to be dipped into bowls of honey. The dates were sweet, too sweet for Blackmore's palate, but he ate two to be polite, marveling that Adnan ate the dates sweetened further with honey.

As they settled back on the cushions to savour the strongly brewed Arabic coffee, Blackmore turned to his host. "I passed the caravansary earlier today, Adnan. Is it still in use?"

"No, my friend. The French built a road over the Atlas Mountains that separate us Moroccans who live on the coast, from the vastness of the Sahara. It has greatly decreased the time it takes for goods to reach our ports. Perhaps you can make that journey. The mountains are spectacular. Not to mention our great city of Marrakesh that lies between Casablanca and Zagora. A few Europeans have begun to travel inland and I understand they find the whole experience charming."

"I would love nothing better, Adnan. But I must get back to London to complete our arrangements. On my next trip I will definitely allow time."

Late that night standing in the shower in his hotel room, Blackmore discovered there was no hot water. Millions of people from the first world now traveled and, Charles reasoned they would spend freely in the less-developed countries if they didn't have to suffer such hardships. This idea was the first brick in the wall of his future. He had gone home and secured Lord Pembroke's help.

The first glimmer of Aruban sunrise disturbed Blackmore's reverie. He had fallen asleep on the sofa. The clock on the TV read 6:08; he was scheduled to leave on the eleven o'clock flight to New York. He didn't feel like being alone in the breakfast room surrounded by happy, vacationing couples, so he picked up the phone and ordered coffee and a croissant to be sent to his room. The sun was now streaming in through the windows and Blackmore was content.

But after checking out of the hotel, there was one last thing he decided to do. He drove to the office of the local police chief, Juan Garcia. The two men had met when Blackmore was contracted to set up his container loading operation. In the container business there was always the potential for insiders to reap great profits by concealing drugs in among the thousands of containers that literally drifted around the world each day. The chief had convinced himself Mr. Blackmore wasn't interested in getting richer illegally and told him so. Today, Blackmore knew he could count on being granted the small favor he wanted: To know the exact moment Prudence Howard left Aruba, and what flight she was on to where.

Prudence Howard

Aruba

One night Ovelia and I were sitting on the porch-swing after cooking a curry together. Actually, Ovelia had instructed me on how to make the Indonesian dish that had been in her father's family since the days when distant relatives worked for the Dutch East India Company. We'd eaten it with Dutch beer, to keep the heat from the spices from burning our mouths.

It had been two weeks since I moved in with her. We occasionally got on each other's nerves, as is usual for two women living together, but, truthfully, this was the closest I'd been to any female in a long, long time.

Ovelia was a competent, smart woman who was willing to risk the unknown.

I'd come to see the strength of the two races from which she sprang; the stoic Dutch sea captain mingling with perhaps a brave Masai warrior who could never be enslaved, who died in captivity, according to Isak Dinesen in her marvelous book, *Out of Africa,* if such a thing were tried.

As we drank tea from cups, blue like the cornflowers my mother used to grow in window boxes outside our hotel in Whistler, we could hear laughter from the boat basin below. Then music rose up the hill in gusts on the light breeze; one person was playing guitar and male voices were trying only marginally successfully to sing the harmonies to *Sloop John B* as the Beach Boys had done it. At least these tourists knew the words.

"Sometimes I wonder how I got to be so lucky," Ovelia said, after explaining how everything at her shoe plant was falling into place. "I had the best father and I have three sons I adore. Now a business that seems to want to create itself."

I wished for her sake that life would allow her to remain in this beatific state but suspected that it wouldn't be so. Few are spared troubles forever. "The harder you work, the luckier you get, my dad used to say. But, you know, I think I have to add a codicil to that." I bit into one of Ovelia's chocolate chip cookies. "You have to work hard to take advantage of opportunities, but you can never be sure you'll get the result you're looking for. Lots of people have worked tirelessly and things have still gone off the rails." I washed down the cookie with a sip of tea. "Actually, my dad was one of those guys."

"Pru, you've been here a few weeks now, but you never talk about yourself, your past." She stirred some more sugar into her tea and took a sip. "I know you're from Canada, but I don't even know where in Canada."

"I was born in Vancouver, British Columbia."

"That's on the west coast, right?"

"Yes. But then when I was in my late teens we moved to Whistler. In the late 1970's the provincial government decided to build a destination ski resort; to create a village like Aspen or Vail that would appeal to the well-heeled international skier."

"I'm not a skier and even I've heard of Whistler. But why would your government build a ski resort?"

"They figured it would bring lots of revenue into the province. Everyone in Vancouver with a flair for making money, or who aspired to be a real estate developer, jumped on the bandwagon. That included my parents.

"My dad, Bill, has the gift of the gab, as the old saying goes. He can talk anyone into investing in his schemes. The problem was he'd keep them afloat by adding more and more investors when cash flow got tight, much to my mother's chagrin. But this time, even my mom and I thought his plan for investing in real estate was solid. It had to be good because it had the word 'real' right in its name.

"While my parents built the hotel, I studied English Literature in Vancouver, going up on weekends and holidays when I wasn't overloaded with papers to write.

"The hotel was small, forty rooms, but it had a bar and a small bistro-style restaurant. Very charming. The Hotel Chaumiere Whistler, they called it, because its roof looked like a thatched cottage from the French Alps. People loved it. It was on the main pedestrian-only street in the town and tourists who weren't even staying there stopped to take pictures.

"My mother ran the bistro. My father looked after the bar and, after I finished school, I became the front desk manager and filled in when I was needed everywhere else. I cleaned rooms, mixed drinks, even cooked if I had to."

"So much for your literature degree." Ovelia bent over and picked off a cactus flower that had finished blooming. "But you must have enjoyed doing something practical after all those years with your nose in a book."

"The front desk was the biggest challenge. The complaints. But I became extremely good at settling people down. 'What is it you'd like me to do?' I'd ask, in my most compassionate voice. Oddly, 'nothing,' was the most usual answer."

"Why did the guests complain if they didn't want you to do anything?"

"I guess being dissatisfied makes some people feel important. I played a game with myself. How long would it take me to calm a guy down and still let him feel that he had shown his girlfriend how important he was? My record was fifteen seconds."

Ovelia laughed. Then noticing one of the tea lights lined up along the deck railing flickered and went out, she retrieved another from a tin box, lit it and put it in place. Then she poured us more tea.

"Living in a ski village must have been great. Were you a skier before you went there?"

"I hadn't been an athlete of any kind, but I got some equipment and hired a coach everybody called Super Dan. He managed to teach me to make wide 'S'turns all the way down the easier runs without falling, but no amount of coaxing would get me to try the steeper slopes. I was content to watch Dan work his way down, his knees bending up to his chest.

"I never had enough confidence or strength and truthfully, I didn't enjoy it enough to want to work at getting in shape. What I did have, though, were fantasies about Super Dan, negotiating his tight little butt into my bed, but he preferred a blond ski instructor who could, on a good day, beat him down the mountain."

"Ah, Pru...that's awful."

"I consoled myself by inventing a reason to never have to ski again. It was a complete genius move in more ways than one. I avoided my horror of steep runs, and didn't have to watch Super Dan romance the lovely Barbara. While waiting at the front desk for guests to arrive or check out, I created stories. Before long I was on a roll with the writing and the front desk duties were getting in the way. I considered telling my folks that Whistler was no longer a good place for me, but my mother decided that for all of us."

"What do you mean?"

"She was skiing mid-week, looking incredibly cute in her white ski suit, white boots, white gloves, and white rabbit-fur earmuffs, when a merchant banker, Lawrence Gilchrist, from Chicago, fell madly in love with her.

"'Do you want to come with me, Pru?' Mother asked, after the guy had persuaded her to run off with him. I declined. My dad needed someone to look after him."

"Weren't you angry with your mom?"

"Not really. I'd like to think there are universal morals, but I've seen enough to know that's not the case. So, I tried not to judge her. My dad's a great guy, charming as I said, but when I stopped to think about their relationship, I wondered why she'd ever married him. My mother's an intellectual. Cultured. My dad never misses a hockey game on TV. I guess by the time she met Lawrence, my dad's charm had worn off. She wasn't cut out to run a bistro. She was more at home being served in a five star restaurant. Lawrence had enough money to provide the good life and he shared her interest in the arts. He likes to spend time in Florence.

"I was never sorry I stayed. As it turned out my Dad did need me. The hotel did okay for a while, but he took to telling all our guests in the bar his sad tale. He was so depressed he began to drink along with them. Then he forgot to ask them to pay. By this time the staff in the restaurant figured out no one was watching the till. I blamed myself for that at first, but eventually I realized I couldn't watch everything. We tried to sell before the bank foreclosed, but it didn't happen."

"Oh, what an awful story. Your poor dad. He must have been really devastated. First he lost his wife to another man, and then the hotel."

"The worst part was when the receivers came. They took everything that wasn't nailed down and sold it to pay our creditors. I hated those people. They were so smug. Heartless. The boss was this blond woman who obviously relished participating in the destruction of our lives. She took every bed, every sheet, every fucking toothpick, even our personal stuff, while we stood by silently and watched.

"'Sorry, Pru,' was all my father could think of to say. I told him it was okay. And it was. Really. What I wanted was to get something published. It was time to let my dad sort out his own life.

"Friends drove us to Vancouver where he stopped to make a new life. I emptied my bank account – the only thing the receivers didn't touch because I didn't own any part of the hotel – and flew to Europe. I asked my mom to put a word in for me with her school chum, Sid, and he eventually got my first two books published in Canada."

Ovelia poured more tea. "That's a great achievement. Doesn't it usually take a long time to get a book published? I've heard writers paper their walls with rejection notices."

"They were minor successes only, not much in the way of royalties. When my savings started to run out, I became anxious. I could have worked in a hotel, but I didn't want to be distracted from the writing. I was learning a lot. My latest story is my best, I think. Then, miraculously, the solution appeared."

"What happened?"

"I met and lived with...well, three men, the last one being Yves. They worked, I wrote."

"Yves?"

"Yes, a wine exporter who loved to spoil me with jewelry and luxury hotels. I traveled with him all over the world."

"Where is Yves now?"

"I had to end it. He was getting serious, wanted to get married. But, I wasn't in love with him. He was great. Just not 'the one'. You know, Ovelia. You're divorced." She stared into the bottom of her teacup. I couldn't imagine her ever doing what I had done. She had been married and now she had a real job while I lived off the kindness of strangers. I expected to see disgust on her face.

She looked up. "I understand. I think I fell out of love with Aston, my husband. Or maybe I was never truly in love. But never mind that, what happened next?"

"Like I said, my money was running out so I took the gold bracelets, diamond earrings, and silver chains – and sold them. I took the bus to Monaco and wrote until that money was almost gone. I was about to find a job in a hotel. Then I met Carlo."

"I think you were very brave to be on your own in Europe, living off your wits like that. You were willing to do anything to get the time you needed to follow your passion."

"Wits, is that a new word for sex, Ovelia?"

We both doubled over in fits of laughter. I'll never forget that moment. She could have judged me for my choices, but she took the high road, offering me an honourable excuse for how I lived.

The next morning I got a call from Sid Cosgrow. "They love your book, Pru. Get the rest to me right away."

"What, are you kidding?"

"No, I'm not kidding. I love it, too. You did great. This one'll be bigger than the others."

I didn't dare tell him I had two more chapters to finish. Ovelia sat up with me the whole night, proofing and correcting as I wrote. In the morning she rushed it to the airport while I fed the kids and got them out the door to school. Then I collapsed into bed. My dreams were full of a man trying to kill me. And the man was Charles Blackmore.

Prudence Howard

Toronto, 1986

Many months later I was sitting behind a polished desk in the centre of a new Spenser's Books on Bay Street in Toronto, just down from the stock exchange. My novel was selling well in Canada now, too, as well as in the states. Money, more money than I had ever made, was being deposited into my bank account every month. It was a heady feeling. And characters were developing into ideas for another book. I couldn't stop smiling.

"The rep figures we'll get brokers leaving work, all the commodity traders," said Sid Crossgrow as he flopped into the chair beside me.

I remembered those brokers from my Whistler days. "What if no one in Toronto cares about endangered species in Africa? Or making money on illegal arms deals?"

"They will. You've made a very believable story about a woman who helps to stop the bad guys. Even guys who make their living off the market have some conscience left."

I was almost reassured.

But they did come, despite my doubts. A line of them. I felt a rush of adrenaline as I looked up into smiling faces saying, "To whom should I dedicate this?" until my smile became frozen in place. I had never considered the down side to fame.

The line was finally coming to an end and I had quit smiling at the new faces when a man wearing a sleek gold watch handed me a book. I looked into the eyes of Charles Blackmore.

My worst nightmare. How did he know I was here? This is bad, very, very bad. I suddenly felt like the thief I had portrayed him to be. I was making money using his life and I hadn't asked his permission. It flashed into my mind that I was doing what I said all rich people did. I was unethical.

"When you're done here, let's go for a drink. I've been wanting to talk to you."

I just bet you have. You've recognized yourself in my book. The problem was: what if the real Blackmore was doing all the evil things I have Bentley Tyler doing under the cover of a container business? Bentley Tyler murdered people. What if Blackmore was as ruthless as I portrayed Tyler to be?

I could feel perspiration wetting my silk shirt. Why would a busy guy like Blackmore want me to sign his book? What was he really doing here? *This is just great. Here I am, about to be famous, and this guy shows up. But surely he's too sophisticated to kill me himself. He could have had someone else do it. Maybe he's just going to threaten a huge lawsuit unless I take my book off the market.*

All this was going through my head as I heard him say, "I'll be back to get you at six."

I was about to protest when he continued, "I've cleared it with your agent. He says you're free until seven-thirty when you two are having dinner with someone from Book-of-the-Month Club."

It was no wonder that a person with his attention to detail made money. He left nothing to chance. Just went for what he wanted. Sure enough, there he was at one minute to six. He whisked me off to his waiting car and we headed uptown.

"I have a favorite little place. Small, charming, easy to talk."

"Sure," I said. I could hear the bad news anywhere.

It was small. It was charming. Booths with high backs so the conversations could stay intimate. What would I like to drink before life as I knew it was over? The money gods were getting even with me for the evil way I had used men.

We sat across from each other. When our eyes met I could feel a heat between us. *He is gorgeous.* I wanted him to touch me. He kept nervously stroking his middle finger with his thumb and that was as charming as the place. *I guess he's going to break it to me slowly. I've got to be careful. Not drink too much. I need to have my wits about me.*

He talked of some business he had done in Mongolia, about the people he'd met there. His interest seemed genuine. I was warming to him in spite of my fears. I began to relax, to enjoy myself. Was I feeling the nervousness of attraction, or were my instincts telling me to be afraid?

Amidst the buzz from the chatter of the other patrons he said, "I'm sorry I have to leave early tomorrow. I've enjoyed seeing you again."

He hasn't said anything threatening. "Uh huh, me too."

"I was thinking....perhaps when the book signing tour is finished, you could come over to France. I have to be in Brittany in a month. There's a great auberge in Pont Aven where I always stay. I know I'm being very forward. You hardly know me. But, you see, I'm a busy man, Pru. I make decisions quickly. You look frightened. I don't mean to frighten you." He reached across the table and gently placed his hand on mine.

"Brittany. Yes, I like the coast there. But, my book. What did you think of my book? How did you know about the signing?"

"I have a large staff. They keep me informed."

"Have you read it?"

"No, sorry." He colored slightly. "I'll read it on the plane tomorrow."

Well, reading it ought to change your mind about seeing me for a cozy weekend. "Why don't you call me in a few days. I'll have a better handle on my schedule." I was sure that he would never call after he finished the book. Or, I would get the threats I had expected after he did.

He dropped me at my hotel and was gone.

For the next few days, I was like the proverbial cat on a hot tin roof. I watched every shadow. Jumped at unexpected noises. Started every time my phone rang. And then after a few days of this neurotic behavior Charles was on the other end of the line. "Hi, I've finished your book."

I felt like a lamb I'd seen on a market day in Morocco. It was a warm, sunny morning and it stood looking around, seemingly happy enough to be in the middle of all the activity, unaware that when it was taken inside the abattoir, it would be the next one to have its throat slit.

Charles Blackmore

As the Concorde taxied out to the runway, Blackmore wondered again what it was about Prudence Howard that attracted him. There had been others...better looking others. Latterly he recalled the alluring bodies he had been intimate with, bodies that seemed to have been sculpted by a professional's knife. Prudence Howard had a great body, he'd seen her naked in front of Carlo's villa, but it was more than that. He liked the feel of her skin, smooth and fine grained. That was essential, but it was more than just physical attraction... she was passionate about saving endangered animals. Passionate about something other than finding a man to take care of her. Perhaps that was it.

He stared at the cover of the book. *A Good Night for Murder* she'd called it. The cover was a moonlit shot of the African savannah in a sepia color with her name as author in red. He opened to the first page and was about to begin reading when the blond flight attendant smiled down on him seductively. She was pretty, with a row of large, even teeth, red lipstick with a darker pencil line outlining full lips. Soft brown eye shadow emphasized bright blue eyes. "Would you like champagne and orange juice, sir?" She pressed her slim hip into the seat in front of him, accentuating the line of her body, and placed the drink on his tray so he couldn't help but notice she wore no wedding ring.

She straightened. "Charles and Diana sat in these seats last week."

"Really?" Blackmore stirred his drink. A pained look crossed his face. He wanted this woman to leave him alone.

But she didn't. She leaned into the seat again and said, "Are you going home or away on business?"

"Home."

"Do you live in London?"

"Yes, I do."

"How fortunate. You know, I just started to fly this route. It will be my first time in England. Have you got any recommendations of what I should see or do?" She reached up and twisted her large gold earring, waiting for a response.

It was all so transparent. He wiped his hand over his face suddenly feeling weary. The few suggestions he gave created no interest when she realized he wasn't to accompany her, so he said, "Look, I have work to finish before I land, so please excuse me."

She looked offended but forced a professional smile and was gone.

He settled back with his drink and continued reading. In his mind's eye he saw Prudence Howard's face, her intense green eyes, the aquiline nose leaning over her keyboard and pounding out this story. He heard the deep throaty tone of her voice, remembered her perfume, earthy with musk. He wondered what rituals she performed, as she got ready for bed. Did she have a long, luxurious bath with lots of bubbles, or did she quickly shower and crawl into bed with her favorite book? Did she eat junk food, or was she fastidious about eating everything fresh. He wanted to know everything about her.

He threw back the drink and forced himself to concentrate on the story. The action started immediately with a young woman, Katherine Vogel, on safari. She and her guide come upon a dead rhinoceros with its horn removed. Deeply moved, Vogel seeks out the authorities and is told it is quite usual for poachers to commit such acts as the horns are worth a good deal of money on the black market. Then Prudence introduces the love interest, Bentley Tyler. Blackmore is amused to see that Tyler is a thinly veiled version of himself: the same black hair and build, and, he is in the container shipping business.

Soon it is obvious to everyone but the heroine that Bentley Tyler is not as he appears. He is, in fact, the villain, using his business to sell illegal arms and the rhino horns. He will stop at nothing to make his fortune.

Blackmore chuckled to himself. She had made it credible that someone in his position had the means to do such foul deeds. He didn't mind, even though it put the container business in a negative light. This was art and he appreciated the clever way she incorporated it into her story.

But the plane had landed and he would have to wait until the end of the day to find out how it all turned out. As he walked out of the jet way in Heathrow he assumed the persona he had created for his business life, that of the courteous, competent Canadian. All his activities fit into neatly organized compartments, each to be opened at the appropriate time. He would think of Prudence no more until her name appeared in his Day Timer and then he would give her a call. But after a week of work on the Mongolian deal he noticed that somehow Prudence Howard had reached under his protective cover and stirred in him a longing for connection. Charles Blackmore sighed. A deep, long sigh. To love and be loved was a natural desire. He had to believe in the possibility of fulfilling that need.

Carlo Minelli

Aruba

Carlo was sitting on his verandah. He gulped at the wine in his glass, too angry to savour its flavor. He had just learned from one of his Aruban staff that since leaving his employ a few months ago, Ovelia Steinmetz had been creating her own shoe business. That woman is more trouble than I could ever imagine, he thought. And it is I, Carlo, who gave her a job so she could support her three boys. She dares to steal my ideas? Start her own atelier? The orange reflection of the setting sun formed a seamless whole with the brilliant light of the sky but he refused to respond to the exquisite beauty. He had ordered his favorite pasta dish, Napolitano, to begin his meal. Anything to feel in control again.

"Where is my dinner? Andre," he called to his steward.

"It is coming, sir. I know it is no excuse, but it is the new chef's first day. He will be more prompt, I'm sure. He comes highly recommended."

At that moment the chef entered the room, his white uniform immaculate. He carried a steaming plate that he placed with assurance on the table. Carlo took a breath of the herbs he adored, about to enjoy a mouthful.

"What is this?" he screamed. Macaroni tubes swam in the red sauce. '"You idiot." Carlo stood up knocking his chair over, his face blushing purple under his tan. With one quick movement he grabbed the plate off the table and flung it violently onto the wooden floor. "I don't eat macaroni." He turned to Andre who stared wide-eyed. "Call my car. I'll dine in a restaurant that has a proper chef."

As Carlo stormed out of the room the young chef asked, "What did I do? What's wrong with these noodles?"

Andre shrugged his shoulders, "I don't know. I've never seen him like this." They left the room in search of the housekeeper who would clean up the mess.

An iguana scampered onto the porch from the top of a bush where he had been absorbing the warmth of the setting sun and began to lick at the red sauce. Such a large feast was a rare treat.

Ovelia Steinmetz

Aruba, 1986

Ovelia studied the legal documents spread across her desk. Carlo Minelli had launched a lawsuit against her company. She picked up the phone and dialed the number for Prudence Howard's hotel in California.

"Pru, hi. It's me, Ovelia."

"Hi, kiddo. How are things?" Prudence had almost fallen asleep again as she watched Good Morning America, regretting last night's second bottle of wine. She had a book signing in an hour.

"Well, great at the plant, but Carlo has filed a lawsuit against me."

Prudence became instantly alert. "What for?" She clicked off the TV.

"He's claiming that I stole his design techniques. The suit is about intellectual property. A patent on an idea. My lawyer told me the burden of proof is on me to convince the judge that I didn't."

"What an asshole. Can you do that? Did you borrow any of his ideas?"

"No. That part will be easy. My shoes are practical. Sexy, but with a small wide heel that allows you to be comfortable walking on cobblestone streets, uneven wooden docks. Even the sand."

"Sounds perfect for the cruise ship trade."

"I had in mind middle-aged, happily married women, long past the time when they have to endure muscle cramps and sore feet to catch a man."

Prudence giggled. She thought of the contented-looking women she'd seen getting off cruise ships with their Tilley-hatted husbands, neither of whom had even dreamed of having an exciting night in bed for years. "Your shoes are sure to be big sellers, Ovelia. Carlo must know they're aimed at a different market. Why would he go to the trouble of suing you? Is he that angry?"

"Perhaps. The wording on the affidavit is deliberately vague, calling the cause for action 'design techniques.' My lawyer thinks he may be doing it just to cause me grief. But, some of my staff did work for Carlo. He trained them to tan the leather. That's where it gets a bit tricky for us. I have to show that those techniques are quite widespread. We've sent a man to Italy to do some research."

"Whoa, that can't be cheap."

"No, but it has to be done. Which brings me to the reason for my call, Pru. You're just about finished your month of book-signings, right?"

"Right. Sid has set up some more in Europe. English editions only, but that won't be for a while."

"Wow, that *is* exciting news." Ovelia stared down at the documents. Part of her wanted to ask Pru more questions about book sales, but she was too absorbed by the enormity of the action set against her. She was still unable to believe it was happening. Carlo was fabulously wealthy. He had fame, so could this be just a power trip? "I have a favor to ask, Pru."

"Ask away. If I can do it, it is yours. I owe you a lot."

"My lawyer thinks it would be advantageous if you could appear in court to testify to the repulsive nature of the work being done in Carlo's factory."

"When would you need me?"

"That's the problem...in two days."

"I'll be there. But will my testimony be enough to convince a judge?"

"It isn't the main argument, but it will help. Our main point is that my staff can swear our shoes are different. Unlike the hand carved wooden heels that is Carlo's design signature, mine are plastic that simulate the look of wood. It was the perfect answer for an island with out-of-work refinery workers. I brought in a guy from the states who taught a couple of my staff to make plastic. We don't use the endangered rare tropical trees that Carlo so prizes."

"That's a plus, Ovelia. I mean on two counts. Your dad would have been proud of you, I'm sure, for helping to keep jobs on the island and I agree with you that anything we can do to save endangered species is important."

"It's a point of satisfaction with me even though I know that only a few trees are used to make the thousands of wooden heels Carlo needs. But, nonetheless, the plastic heels are my design and I'm sure I can convince the judge that my shoes are completely different from the Minelli brand."

Pru looked at her watch. "I need to run. I'll let you know my arrival time."

"Bye, Pru. And, thanks."

Ovelia hung up. Oh, I forgot to tell her, Charles Blackmore will be here too, she said to herself as she smoothed her sleeked-back chignon with both hands making sure there were no errant ends and straightened her suit jacket. Blackmore's an associate of Carlo's. Maybe he's coming here to spy on my operation, get some inside info for Carlo's side. Even though Charles has been a family friend for years, could he have a greater loyalty to Carlo than to me? I'll have to be cautious in case Mr. Blackmore is really the blue beard Pru made him out to be in her novel.

She pressed her glossed lips together and turned once more to the legal documents. What was most startling and potentially financially devastating was that Carlo had his expensive Italian lawyers place a certificate of pending litigation on all her property, effectively freezing her assets, including her family home, to pay for the damages Carlo expected to receive when he won. I have children. Aruba is my home. Where would I go if I sold everything before the trial? It was a tactic the lawyers used, she knew, to make her nervous. It made her angry. His timing was awful. She'd been arranging financing for the business but when the bank found out about the pending lawsuit they declined to advance the loan. Damn him. This business will give my children the financial security they deserve.

She wanted her lawyer to ask for a special hearing to remove the certificates but he informed her that Carlo's action was a completely legitimate, a tactic to encourage her to settle. It was then that she knew she would fight to the death. She hadn't done anything wrong and she would never admit she had. It was how she'd been raised.

Ovelia laid her head back against the chair and closed her eyes. She thought of the men she'd loved. Her father, of course. He was stern but thoughtful, always there for her and always expecting the best from her, which she was only too pleased to do. Then there was her husband. Aston had loved her and abandoned her. No, she thought, that's not exactly right. They had abandoned each other and now he was somewhere in Ethiopia and she was raising their boys alone. She thought of Carlo and felt the familiar rush of excitement. My God, even with him suing me, I still have feelings for the guy. She opened her eyes and sat upright in her chair. I can't let my feelings make me lose focus.

Prudence Howard

Aruba, 1986

The next day Ovelia picked me up from the airport at 7:00 as the setting sun was turning the shadows a deep purple. The small French restaurant, Martine's, on the beach where we stopped for dinner, was famous for its cuisine; the escargot was cooked in real butter and the chocolate mousse was made with real eggs and full-fat cream. My body soaked it up. The food in California, where I'd spent the last few days at signings, keeps Hollywood stars from adding an ounce of weight to their tall frames, but it chilled my Canadian bones. I like real, old-fashioned food; reject anything the manufacturers call edible that's made in a lab. Whatever they put in low-fat yoghurt or salad dressings can't be good for you. The piano player was hammering out Beatles' tunes to a funky jazz rhythm all his own. Ovelia and I could talk without being overheard.

"What do you mean Charles Blackmore is here for the trial? Does he know I'm here?" When the arrangements were being made I hadn't thought to ask Ovelia about him and I'd been too busy with the book signings to worry about his reaction to my book.

"I told him. He seems anxious to see you."

"I bet." I took a large gulp of wine. *I want to see him as much as I want to get old and wrinkled.*

Ovelia stopped eating. "I think he likes you. What's wrong with that?"

"If he's read my book, he'll realize that Bentley Tyler is modeled after him. Has a shipping business just like Blackmore. And, you remember, Ovelia, I made him evil, a really unethical businessman who traffics in drugs and other illegal stuff."

"I've known Charles for a long time, Pru. He isn't someone who would be upset you used him to stimulate your imagination. I doubt that he would feel threatened. He knows what fiction is."

"But what if he *is* crooked? He might be very upset that I've blown his cover."

A look of horror came over Ovelia's face. She remembered her own doubts about Charles's loyalty. "Oh, I'm so sorry I've brought you here."

I emptied my wine glass. "I wouldn't have missed it. You're doing a really important thing, fighting Carlo. He's a control freak. You can't let that ruin your chances of making a very good business." *I shouldn't be worrying Ovelia when she needs to keep her wits about her.* "But, you're probably right about Blackmore. He's obviously just crazy about me and will do anything to see me again."

We grinned at each other, as I broke a piece of French bread and dipped it into the garlic butter left on the escargot plate. "Tell me about the trial preparations and let's forget my paranoia."

"My lawyers have thought of everything, right down to the detail of measuring shoe heel diameters with calipers."

"What do you want me to do?"

"Just testify as to why you quit." Ovelia stopped eating, apparently to ponder what she had just said, her forehead wrinkled and her mouth formed into a deep frown. "This is really asking a lot of you. I don't want to be responsible for you and Charles having a run in. I know him, but I don't *really* know him." She looked up. "Maybe you should just go on to London."

Part of me wanted to run. The chicken part. But, I couldn't. Supporting Ovelia in her fight against Carlo was important. I had to see it through. And, for once, it was not just about me. *It's putting an indelible mark on my character, a positive mark. Besides, what's the worst that could happen? He could kidnap and torture me, meticulously cut my body into little pieces, then, toss them into the sea from the huge crane that moves all those containers on the loading dock, just like I'd had Bentley Tyler do to people who crossed him.*

Get a grip, Pru, I said to myself. Your writer's brain is probably making the whole thing up. You need to keep your sense of humor or at least sense of proportion. If he did cut you up into little bits and disposed of the pieces, to whom would he be sending a warning? It is highly unlikely that any of the little old ladies reading my book would relate my antagonist to Charles Blackmore. Besides, my story in no way proves he's a real life villain. But no matter how I tried to rationalize the situation, I couldn't get the thought out of my head he *would* care a great deal about his cover being blown if that's what I'd done.

"No, I can't run. I'll see this through to the end." I smiled at Ovelia and dunked another piece of bread into the butter. "It's part of my Canadian character. We believe ourselves to be good."

"Well, Charles is Canadian, too, right?"

I stopped in mid-bite and laughed uproariously. "Right. By definition he simply couldn't be a bad guy." I said it, but I knew the image was false. Canada has jails just like every other country.

The next day, court wasn't in session until after lunch, so in the morning, I went to Ovelia's workshop. The cab headed west to the site of the former refinery. About twenty cars were parked in front of the only building that looked occupied.

I found Ovelia leaning over a large, slightly battered table inspecting some plants. She was wearing a long shift with large blocks of cobalt blue stamped in various shapes over a yellow background, her tall, slim frame accentuating the line of the dress. She looked like a walking piece of abstract art, but she still managed to evoke the image of a powerful and sexy businesswoman.

She handed me a latte in a Styrofoam cup. "We're going to use this madder plant. It's an ancient source of natural red dye. It'll be our signature color. The plant loves the climate here. I've experimented. The desert conditions are perfect and cultivating it will provide more jobs. Well," she looked solemn for just a second, "just a few jobs. But, I'm so excited."

"This place is a big deal," I said as I waved my hand around the room, indicating the office and the manufacturing plant. "And it's only been five months."

"I've always had an eye for design. Art was my favorite subject in school," Ovelia said. "I have to admit, if I hadn't worked for Carlo, I couldn't have done this. I learned a lot about running a fashion business. I owe him that."

"It might be best not to volunteer that in court."

"You're right. But people do learn things while they work for others. That can't be illegal." She looked up, questioning the truth of her statement, and then went on, "besides, it's just that shoes really speak to me. I have a closet full of them."

I looked at her feet. She was wearing a pair of sandals that matched the blue in her dress.

"Do you like these? They're my design."

Elasticized blue fabric covered the top of her foot, exposing enameled toenails. The heels were broad, square. The effect was smart and practical. "They're great."

Ovelia said, "I remember the day I was walking down Front Street and a pair of black sandals caught my eye. The curve of the heel was similar to the shape of Greek vases I loved to look at in my father's art history books. So precise. The tension... oh, it's so hard to explain. It's like the way Nature curves a pear. If it was less extreme it would be dull, and more extreme it would be rococo. Busy. In Nature there is some exact mathematical formula that makes things just perfect and we humans recognize it. It's what we refer to as beauty. Am I making any sense?" She held her hands out, pleading.

"Yes, perfect sense."

"Well, when I tried those shoes on, my feet felt utterly feminine. I know that sounds crazy, but it's true."

"If they were Carlo's shoes, I know *exactly* what you mean. The man is a genius."

"They were. But what I don't understand about Carlo is, how can a man who is capable of creating such beauty, someone who puts such soul into his work, be the same man who can slaughter innocent creatures?" She paused to contemplate her question for a few seconds.

"Then a few days later I noticed an ad in *Aruba Today*. Minelli Shoes was looking for someone to manage a branch plant soon to be opening here. Carlo thought the job was so important, he did the interviewing himself. When I walked into the room and looked at him, I was smitten. I had never met a man so sophisticated, so charming. I had to get that job. I wracked my brain for an idea that would impress him.

"I suggested that he should not just do the tanning here. His labour costs would be cheaper if he trained Arubans to dye the skins as well. I knew the locals would be happy with a lesser pay rate because it's cheaper to live here than in Italy. But I also figured if the finishing work was done in Italy – the cutting of the leather, the sculpting of the wooden heels, the assembly – then the 'Made in Italy' stamp could still be displayed, something that's vital to Carlo's marketing strategy."

"Carlo was obviously impressed with your business head."

"The problem was I was so taken with the elegant Mr. Minelli, I didn't ask what he had in mind. That night when I opened a bottle of wine with one of my girlfriends to celebrate, I was assuming the skins would come from Italy."

"That was reasonable. Who would have thought he was going to use the iguanas?"

"That day you first arrived in Aruba and I ran past you in the hall..."

"Yes, I remember."

"Carlo and I had had an argument. I told him the iguana is important to Arubans. To him they're nothing but a combination of snake and rodent, a pest the island would be well rid of." Ovelia took a sip of her latte. "He didn't care that Aruba is the only place in the world they exist. To him the only good thing about them was the use he could make of the interesting pattern of their skins."

"A lot of people are morbidly afraid of fast-moving little creatures. Maybe Carlo's one of them. He was right about the skins. They look beautiful dyed."

Ovelia's face fell.

"Sorry, Ovelia. I'm not siding with him. It's just that what makes me able to write my characters with depth; get into their heads, is that I'm very good at seeing things from the other person's point of view. I understand why people do the things they do."

She smiled at me. "I know. I've read your book."

"I'm not really myself today," I said.

"Why not?"

"I was awake from about three on. I read somewhere writers are some of the most depressed people. I had one of my nightmares. It was about a young boy being tortured."

"Oh, that's awful."

"It was, actually. And every time I started to fall asleep, the dream would start up again. I had to force myself to stay awake. Usually I scream out loud when I have these dreams. Yves was the best at waking me up and getting me to think of something else."

Ovelia looked quizzical.

"You remember Yves. The man I lived with just before I met Carlo."

"Yes, the wine merchant, right?"

"Uh-huh. He'd wake me up gently, hold me and talk to me about something nice. Some place we'd been, or a great meal we'd shared, until I fell asleep again. With his arms around me the dream usually didn't start up again. But when I'm alone, like last night, the dreams return, no matter what I try to think of."

"So we've just discovered one reason to be in a relationship."

We were laughing together again.

"I've been reading some of Carl Jung's writings. I'm especially interested in his ideas of the collective unconscious," I said.

I looked at Ovelia to see if she was tracking with this thought.

She nodded. "I've read him, too."

"Remember his ideas about the archetypes? That they're the personifications of ideas or themes that imply the good or a god."

Ovelia nodded again.

"My dreams are impersonal like that...not just jumbled stuff from my memory bank. They seem most prevalent when I'm delving into the depths of a character. They're always demonic. Stuff happens that I don't even want to contemplate it's so ugly. People are usually trying to kill me. That's why I wake up screaming. Do you think human beings are able to create evil from the depths of our unconscious minds? Is that where evil originates?" I finished my latte and stared at the foam left in the bottom. When I looked up, Ovelia seemed troubled.

"I don't know," she said.

"Oddly, the dream made me think about Carlo. When I first met him, he asked me to have coffee with him on his yacht. He asked if I believed in angels."

"That's interesting."

"I know. He told me that his mother made him draw angels when he was a kid. A gift to her God, he said. But he told me he didn't believe in her religion any longer."

"His yacht's called *Angelita,* isn't it?"

"Yes. Do you think he named it after a specific woman?"

"That would make sense. Maybe he was in love with her. An unrequited love or something like that. Maybe that's why we never hear of him dating anybody."

"Um, could be."

"But it still doesn't explain why he has such a hatred for iguana."

"I don't think we'll ever know. Like I said, maybe it's some kind of innate fear of rodents. Maybe when you fear something enough, you can kill it. Or torture it." I was thinking of my dream again. We sat is silence for a moment just looking at each other. "I had an art history professor who told me an interesting story about his daughter. I had gone to ask him a question about his lecture. In the course of the conversation he told me his daughter lived in London and worked for Amnesty International. It was her job to read all the files that came in about the tortures being committed all over the world. Can you imagine?"

Ovelia's voice was hoarse with emotion. "No, I wouldn't be able to do that."

"He told me that sometimes she would phone. When he said 'hello', she wouldn't say anything. He could hear her sobbing, so he'd just hold the phone and let her cry. When she was done she'd tell him she loved him and they would hang up."

"Maybe we all have some insanity in us." Ovelia straightened a line of pens on her desk. "Actually, I must. How else do I explain working for Carlo as long as I did when I knew what was going on? Love is blind, as they say, but how sick is that? I definitely turned a blind eye to what was happening. Until that day I met you." She looked up at me.

"I remember you running out of his office looking upset."

Ovelia began to break the top of her plastic cup with the edge of her nail. "He has a very bad temper. When he has an idea, he's driven, obsessed. Nothing will turn him off his course." She threw the cup in the waste-paper basket. "He'll go through with this trial. There'll be no settling."

"But if Carlo hadn't come here, you might not have had the idea for this business."

"You're right, I'm grateful for that." She reached out and hugged me. "But Carlo is still killing the iguana. We didn't stop him from doing that. And he continues to pay young island boys to do the killing and bring the carcasses to the warehouse. I feel terrible. I was an accomplice in the destruction of our national treasure. Carlo does it for money he surely doesn't need."

"We shouldn't attribute to money what is really a function of human nature," I said. Money's morally neutral. It's what we do to make it and then how we spend it that's either good or bad, don't you think? Wealth can bring temptations...but then again, so can poverty. I think Carlo loves the power money conveys." I thought of my own selfish deeds. *What is it with Aruba? I keep stumbling into things I don't like about myself here.*

Prudence Howard

Courthouse, Aruba

I was sitting on a long wooden bench at the rear of the courtroom while I waited to testify, observing Carlo. He was a man possessed, his eyes dark, demonic orbs. When I'd first met him, his face was full of life. It wasn't just the appeal of his opulent life-style that had attracted me; I'd wanted to get to know *him*. But I'd forgotten, or wanted not to think about the fact that everyone's psyche has a shadow side.

Blackmore came in and sat down beside me. When he smiled, I felt the heat of attraction, aware of his precisely tailored tropical suit, his finely formed hands resting on his thighs.

My mind replayed all our conversations trying to figure out if he'd ever said anything that would indicate he was intent on harming me. I had to admit he hadn't. But, if he appeared in public with Ovelia and me, helping us, people would remember his supportive smile. Carlo would be the one under suspicion, thought to be angered to the point of deadly revenge for my testifying against him. I fidgeted, crossing first my right leg over the left, than reversing the action. Bentley Tyler would have planned it that way.

I heard my name called and walked to the witness stand. I hoped my voice would not betray the tension I felt.

Pru, you're a knight about to attack with a lance. Now let down your face guard and charge.

One of Carlo's lawyers had round, soft eyes and a slightly balding head that gave him an amiable appearance. "Isn't it true, Ms. Howard, you caused a quarrel between Ms. Steinmetz and Mr. Minelli?" he asked. His voice, aggressive and harsh, as it drove into the silent room, stunned me. I hadn't thought of the events as proceeding exactly that way, but, the part of me that could see it from Carlo's point of view, thought, maybe you did, Pru. Maybe this is entirely your fault. In the pre-trial conference with Ovelia's lawyer, the possibility of this question hadn't come up. My mind was as blank as a mid-August sky, but I knew this was not the time for a meditative calm.

I heard Carlo's lawyer ask me again, "Did you or did you not cause the quarrel between Ms. Steinmetz and Mr. Minelli? Please answer the question."

Think, Pru, think. I felt panicked. I tried to force a thought, any thought into my mind. I looked up to where Blackmore was sitting. He held my gaze, willing me to be calm. Assuring me everything would be fine. Time slowed as my mind reviewed the past. Blackmore's gaze became the still point of the universe where I could think clearly.

"No, I did not."

Barely visible, a small smile appeared at the corners of Blackmore's mouth. Then he released me.

The Italian lawyer's voice deepened. "Tell the court, then, Ms. Howard, why you and Ms. Steinmetz stopped working for Minelli Shoes at the same time."

Each time I gave an answer he asked another question that made me doubt what I had just said. I felt flustered and was making a mess of my testimony. I was too upset to look at Blackmore again. I was now no longer sure what I believed. Finally the judge told me I could step down.

As I returned to my seat I felt defeated. Blackmore reached out and held my hand. His energy was strong, confident, reassuring. I wanted to be wrapped in his arms. But as we sat listening to the rest of the testimony, the niggling question kept going through my mind, "Why is he helping me?"

When the session ended, Ovelia, Blackmore and I left the courtroom together. Ovelia's shoulders drooped. I knew I'd let her down.

Blackmore said, "Ladies, you've had a very demanding day. Allow me to take you for an early dinner at Chez Christophe. It's the best food on the island, don't you agree, Ovelia?" he asked, but he was looking at me.

"I really need a drink. Let's go," Ovelia said.

I could feel the color rising in my face. Even though I felt this strong physical attraction to Blackmore, I didn't have the energy to be with him. The thought went through my mind that I was needlessly mixing up Blackmore with Bentley Tyler, the character I'd created. I had no proof Blackmore was an unscrupulous businessman, but I was absolutely too wrung out to have to deal with my anxiety and suspicions. "I don't feel like eating."

Blackmore said, "I know that lawyers never let you say things as you see them. It's their job. But remember, the judge sees these tactics all the time. I'm convinced he'll rule in your favor, Ovelia. Your shoes are going to be big sellers. I'm here to secure your business, so taking you to dinner is not entirely selfless."

They both looked to me. I could see that Blackmore was trying very hard to make us both feel better. "You two go. I can't. Sorry. I'll see you tomorrow, Ovelia," I said, as I fled the foyer of the courthouse.

Back in my hotel room I lay in the tub, aloe oil soaking into my skin as I pondered how everything had become complicated. Usually my intuition was right about men. Blackmore liked me and honestly, I couldn't see him as a vindictive assassin. I couldn't even see him instigating a lawsuit against me for using the circumstances of his life in my story without his permission. But I couldn't get rid of the feeling that he was hiding something. And it was making me crazy.

I ran more hot water into the deep tub hoping to steam out my irritation, but as I rubbed the face cloth across my arms I knew I hadn't. I felt terrible and I was hungry, a condition which always increased my angst. I got out of the tub, wrapped myself in a thick cotton towel and opened the room service menu. But I was too restless to stay in my room, so I dressed and went down to the patio restaurant and found a table out of the wind that seemed to be getting stronger.

I was downing the last of the grilled scampi when Charles Blackmore walked in. There was nowhere to run.

"May I join you?"

"Yes, of course. But how did you find me?"

"Ovelia."

"Yes, of course." *Ovelia told him where I was? I thought she liked me.*

"She also told me you're afraid of me."

Doomed. "Ovelia told you that? Boy, that's what you

get for coming all this way to help a friend, a so-called friend."

"Relax, Pru. I did see myself in your book. I was flattered, of course, by how good-looking you made me. The rest was just good fiction. Most authors base their characters on someone in real life, correct? Besides, I don't make money transporting drugs or any other illegal items. I have nothing to hide."

I guess he wouldn't say that if he were a crook. "Yes, but do you want my readers to think of you as Bentley Tyler? I mean, aren't you worried people will start asking you how *did* you get so rich so quickly?"

"Realistically, how many of your readers would have heard of me, Pru?"

The waiter silently removed my plate. "I'd like a café Americano. Would you like something, Charles?"

"The same." Blackmore began to drum the table slowly, "And anyone who knows me knows how hard I've worked. They also know I was at the right place at the right time. The container business was just taking off when I got into it. If someone started out today, it would be very difficult to achieve what I did. By working so hard, though, I've..." he looked up, "I've made no time for a personal life."

He paused, clearly wanting acknowledgment I understood what he was getting at. *Ovelia sent him. She must trust him. Is she trying to put two lonely people together? It feels like I just dropped into a bad romantic novel.* I realized Blackmore was still talking.

"I'm here to support Ovelia, just like you, but..." He paused, breaking open a sugar packet and dumping the contents into his cup. A muscle moved along his jaw. "I like her. I'll ship her goods for a more than fair price. I owe that much to her father for all the help he gave me. But, I've really come..."

Charles' difficulty in saying what he wanted to say was endearing. My mind wandered and I visualized him in a tuxedo. Then I imagined him with the suit off. I forced myself to keep listening.

"Look, Pru. The truth is...for the first time," he stopped, seemingly unsure of how to continue. He steadied his breath. "You're different. You worked for Carlo to get the money to keep writing. You had a dream and you kept at it until you achieved your goal. You have no idea how refreshing that is to me. I respect you." His face became even more serious. "I've never respected women who are hangers-on. I respect you, Pru," he repeated. "You and Ovelia. But, I guess you can see...I'm attracted to you. I want you to go away with me."

A feeling of horror was spreading through my body. Blackmore was actually falling for me, but it was a case of mistaken identity. I *am* one of those women he despises. The horror was turning to a sickening feeling in the pit of my stomach. If he knew the truth about me he'd be gone like a shot. I had been a hanger-on. Yes, I wanted to write a successful book, but I would have kept on living with men who could afford to give me a great life if I had found I had no real talent. My mother always told me, "Pru, it's just as easy to fall in love with a man who has money than with a poor guy." I had made sure I put myself in places where I would meet men of means, like Yves. Sometime, if Blackmore and I dated, I would say something, or we'd meet a former lover and I'd have to explain. I wouldn't want to see the look of disappointment on his face when his illusion was shattered. But the really nutty-making part was he had just convinced me he's a guy who worked hard, got lucky, and created millions. He's no Bentley Tyler.

"I need to go. It was great you came by. I enjoyed getting to know you better. But, honestly," and I was telling the truth, "this will never work." And I walked out.

Charles Blackmore

Back in his hotel room Charles pondered what had just happened. He could have sworn there was real chemistry between him and Prudence, but something kept stopping her. "That madman, Carlo, really has these women upset. They're tough, but no one likes to be sued," he said aloud. He dialed Carlo's private number to arrange a meeting.

It was still light as Charles sped down the drive to Carlo's villa.

"*Buona sera*, my friend. Come in." Carlo led the way to the living room. The French doors were closed against a strong wind now blowing from the west, dark clouds denying them a view of the setting sun. The grey-green sea was wild with long streaks of spindrift. Carlo mixed them each a tall gin and tonic.

Blackmore noticed a book-marked copy of Pru's novel on the table in front of him. Interesting, he thought as he nosed his drink, enjoying the earthy smell of the fermented juniper berries. The two men began an easy conversation about long standing associates. Then Blackmore decided it was time to ask the questions he had come to ask.

"What's happening with the atelier here in Aruba, Carlo?"

"I've brought a manager from Italy to oversee the work."

Carlo squeezed the lime into his drink and stirred it with the silver stir stick. "I assure you, Charles, I will not again make the mistake of employing a local manager."

"What is it you're trying to achieve with this trial? Surely it's costing you more than it's worth. You could just drop it."

"She stole from me. I won't allow anyone to do that." Carlo's fingers tightened on the cut-crystal glass until his knuckles whitened.

"But a single woman with three kids. Isn't that a bit..." Charles struggled to find the right adjective. "Unmanly?"

Carlo studied the younger man for a few moments. "I'll tell you what happened to me. Because we are friends."

Blackmore winced at the term "friends". At this moment he felt more like a traitor. He was here to get Carlo to back off.

"I've told you a bit about my early life, no?"

"Yes," Blackmore acknowledged, sipping his drink.

"After my parents died I wanted to go traveling. Find myself, is, I think, the current expression. I leased my farm to the neighbour. The man was like an uncle to me. That I believe I told you."

Blackmore nodded. "You did."

Carlo's face hardened, his jaw muscles working with emotion. "He agreed to pay the mortgage payments on a loan my parents had taken out against the farm to provide my two sisters with dowries. Our arrangement was that any earnings from the farm production would be his. I headed south looking for work, for a life. As I said, he was family. I trusted him."

Carlo slammed his drink violently onto the table, liquid spilling onto his perfectly manicured fingers. His face grew crimson.

"Do you know what that bastard did? He didn't pay the bank." Carlo was breathing heavily, each inhalation rasping, his voice, a noise like thunder. "When the bank couldn't find me, they called the loan. The property was put up for sale. My 'uncle' bought it for twenty cents on the dollar. When I finally found out and confronted him, he claimed we had no deal.

"It had all been done on a handshake. My word against his. Even if I had some proof, I had no money to fight him. By the time I had the means to buy it back...I would have paid whatever he wanted...he had already sold the land. It was turned into a subdivision. I swore on my mother's grave I would never let anyone do that to me again."

Blackmore now understood why Carlo was overreacting to Ovelia opening a business. How could he reason with a man who was confusing the past with the present? He had to give it a shot.

"Look, Carlo, I happen to know Ovelia's in love with you."

"In love? What does she know about love?"

"I've known Ovelia since she was a young girl. She confides in me like a brother since her father died. This business with the iguana, it ripped her apart to confront you. She has real feelings for you."

"Why should I care about that? I will never tarnish the memory of my Angelita by taking another woman. We are the same, Charles. There are women everywhere who pretend to be interested in us, when it's our wealth they're attracted to. Look at the other one, Miss Prudence Howard. She was broke. The night we met, I took her to dinner because I'm always interested in talking to creative people. She admitted to being short of money and offered to sleep with me. I would have sent her on her way, but she happened along when I needed her help. I offered her an income instead of allowing her to prostitute herself. And now that she's newly risen in the world, a parvenu as the French say, she's willing to testify against me," Carlo said with a sardonic laugh indicating the depth of his hatred.

Blackmore was stunned by this revelation, his mind racing. "Did Pru actually offer to sleep with you?" It turned out she was like all the other women he'd known. It was a good thing she'd ended it before it even began...before he made a fool of himself. He stared into the liquid in his glass not wanting Carlo to see he was shaken.

Carlo stood and poured his unfinished drink into the bar sink. "Yes, she did. She was quite drunk by the time we were driving home from dinner. She offered, and then she passed out. I had my crew carry her onto my yacht and place her in the guest cabin. In the morning when I got a call from my office that the advertising agency had let me down, she and I were in the lounge. I'd spent enough time with her to judge her intelligence, so I made her the offer of a job."

The only thing Blackmore knew for sure at this moment was he'd promised Ovelia he would help her win her case. He'd do that and then return to England. He emptied his glass and stood. "I've got to be going, but even though I usually don't give unsolicited advice, you should rethink this legal thing. I like Ovelia and I think underneath it all, you do too. I don't want to see her have to go through this. I know you would never betray your love for Angelita by taking another woman. That's not what I meant. I just wanted to let you know she was wounded by more that just the lawsuit. She was very fond of you." Blackmore paused to give his final statement emphasis. "I think you can understand that kind of angst."

Blackmore put his hand firmly on his friend's shoulder. "The thing with the farm, though. Damn, that's ugly. What a way to lose your family's place."

What Blackmore didn't see as he sped down the drive, was Carlo pouring himself a cognac and while acknowledging that Blackmore had understood his pain, he didn't understand how much better it made Carlo feel to push his pain onto someone else.

As Blackmore drove he turned these revelations about Prudence Howard over in his mind. There was one thing he was clear about. She had penetrated the shell he had erected around his emotions. Fear washed over him. In his business dealings, he pushed through such feelings, focusing his will on what he was after. He'd do that now. Help solve Ovelia's problem.

He pressed the accelerator enjoying the feeling of freedom as the wind rushed through his hair. The faces of women who would have married him in an instant flashed before him, those that had become solicitous when they discovered his vast fortune. He'd dared to hope Prudence Howard would love him for himself.

He passed a car that was going the speed limit, narrowly missing an on-coming car as he swerved back into his lane. In his mind he was rehearsing his next move.

The next afternoon as Blackmore walked out of the pink colonial court building he squinted against the reflection of the Friday afternoon sun bouncing off the harbour. Watching Ovelia's lawyer, a well-intended man who usually acted for small petty criminals on the island, Charles knew the man was out of his league with this case. Ovelia and Pru had taken no pictures of the mutilated iguanas. In their outrage over the slaughter they had simply quit working for Carlo, never thinking he'd sue. In fairness to them, who would have guessed the Italian would have such an intense reaction? But Charles now had a plan that even Ovelia's lawyer couldn't bungle, and to execute it he would need some evidence.

He checked his watch. The janitor at Minelli Shoes would undoubtedly be at the tanning factory, cleaning up after the day's work was over. Blackmore knew from experience that poor people in developing economies were open to bribes. He would pay the man well.

The lights were on as he rang the bell at the front entry. The clipped sound of English spoken by a man who had learned it as his second language came through the metal grille of the door. After Blackmore explained what he needed, he slid a stack of bills through the mail slot. The door opened and he was led to the workroom. The acrid smell of blood and guts overwhelmed him as he entered. It seemed that he had interrupted the janitor shoveling the carcasses into a small handcart.

"What do you do with all...this?"

"I wheels it down to the bay and gives it to the fish for food."

It *was* revolting. Blackmore walked past a table where the rodents had not yet been skinned. Some of them had died with their eyes open and it seemed like they were watching him as he moved across the room. It made the hair on the back of his neck stand up. He realized that making a fashion item out of a wild animal, offended him, too. He took a series of pictures and left, happy once outside to breathe clean salt air.

Ovelia's car was in the driveway when he drove up to her house. "I've got something to help with the case," he said, taking a seat on one of the chintz-covered chairs. Blackmore was feeling good about his plan. It would very likely work, he thought as Ovelia handed him a glass of white wine. "With your permission, I'd like to shake Carlo up a bit."

"Oh? By doing what?"

"I took some pictures of the iguana in Carlo's factory. It's pretty disturbing to see all those dead creatures, especially the ones where the heads are still attached."

"So will you bring them to court? Try to sway the judge?"

"No. I have connections in the publishing business in Europe. They'll be in all papers. We'll let the public be the judge."

"That's brilliant, Charles. Carlo won't want to see his precious name besmirched. After all, the fact Pru and I resigned didn't stop the slaughter, just our hand in it. Maybe some publicity will get him to quit. And," Ovelia paused, "if it's embarrassing enough, he might just forget about the lawsuit."

As arranged, Blackmore met with the publisher of *Aruba Today* to have the pictures sent over the wire. The news coverage won't be enough to destroy him, Blackmore thought, just enough to get his attention; show him that he's really not invincible. The story about his farm is sad, but we've all had people take advantage when we weren't looking. He needs to get over it.

After the last picture was wired, Blackmore returned to his hotel, had a light dinner, a shower, and attempted to sleep. He forbade himself to think of Prudence Howard, but just before he fell asleep her face was there before him.

Prudence Howard

I poured a gin and tonic and walked onto the hotel balcony into the hot night air. *This couldn't be a more awkward situation for me. Blackmore in court every day and now he and Ovelia are doing business together.*

I sat, pulled off my shoes and rested my feet on the other chair. *Rooms are always set up for two. Well, I'm going to get used to being one. I'm giving up men.* I squeezed the lime into my drink and took a sip. *Who am I kidding? The talent gods gave me the ability to flirt with men. It's my gift. I have to use it. Besides, it's such an automatic response for me, the cathedral where I worship. I'll never give up men entirely. Just Carlo and Charles.*

I stood and refilled my glass, taking note that the first one had gone down very quickly. *My father's genes. But this isn't the time to be worried about rotting my liver.*

Back outside, I became aware of the vacationers on a nearby balcony. They were in the midst of an animated conversation. Riotous laughter filled the air. *People having fun. That's what life's all about. I've broken one of my cardinal rules and started taking things too seriously. Look where that's got me.*

A knock came at the door. I jumped involuntarily. *I'm a nervous wreck.*

Through the security window I could see a bellman with an envelope on a silver tray.

"There is a letter for you, Madame."

I read the handwritten note. "On Monday morning check the European papers." Signed, Charles Blackmore.

In the hotel lobby, the front pages of the papers were filled with pictures of slaughtered iguana and the late afternoon ones showed placard-carrying pickets protesting in front of Carlo's elegant boutiques. Women were burning their Minelli's in bonfires set in squares all over Milan.

Oh my god. This is a disaster. I hurried back to my room and rang Blackmore's hotel.

"Charles, it's Pru."

"Hi. Did you get my note?"

"Yes, it's why I'm calling. Look, I'm sure at the moment you feel like a latter-day Savonarola." My voice cracked. "But did it occur to you Carlo might think I broke this story to the media?" I wanted to add, "you moron," but was holding myself back with great effort.

There was a pause on the line and then he said, "No, I hadn't thought of that. Why would he think you did it?"

I could feel my jaw tighten. "Because he hired me to write advertising copy. He gave me a list of all the magazines and newspapers he uses. I could have sent the story to all his contacts. He'll probably sue *me* now. He's in a very litigious frame of mind."

I hung up the phone. I was so angry I didn't want to hear his response.

Carlo Minelli

Aruba

Carlo Minelli sat with newspapers strewn across his desk, their headlines and pictures denouncing him. He was thinking. If they think this will stop me, they're wrong. I am going to root out, utterly destroy Ovelia and anyone who has helped her. I've questioned everyone in the factory, including the night janitor. No one's admitting where these photos came from. But for now, I can't fire them all.

Carlo stood and yanked open the louvered door of his study. The bright light reflecting off the sea caused him to squint, but the sheer beauty of the view forced him to take a deep breath. He reminded himself what a powerful and wealthy man he was, that he had weathered many storms.

Why, he wondered, are people so concerned about the lives of these ridiculous reptiles? Humans have been using the skins of animals for clothing since the beginning of time. It was not so long ago that women would do anything, literally, to get a fur coat, the more exotic the better. But now these animal rights activists are running around the world, stirring up feelings that are better left suppressed. He grimaced, poured a jigger of brandy into the espresso he'd been drinking, and told himself he was just filling a need for beautiful, glamorous things.

The phone rang, interrupting his thoughts. "Carlo, this is Giuseppe. You need to get back here. We haven't sold a shoe in the last two days. You need to make some kind of public statement."

Carlo had been anticipating this call from his VP of Finance. He could feel his blood pressure rising as he thought of the effect this would have on his staff.

"I don't understand what those editors were thinking." Giuseppe's voice rose sharply. "We spend a lot of money in all those papers. Why would they print a story that could ruin us?"

"Obviously selling papers is more important than being loyal."

"This will ruin us, Carlo. Our share price is falling. You need to do something."

"Yes, yes. I'll call you back."

Carlo slammed down the phone. His heart sank as he thought of all his beautiful shoes, so lovingly made by his craftsmen, burned on a pyre like some profane books. He had worked all his adult life to create an empire that brought pleasure to the women who wore his shoes and the men who enjoyed beautiful women. Now his customers had turned on him. He sat on the chaise longue, running his hand over his head. He realized for the first time in a very long while, he was not sure what to do. He began to mull over the facts yet again. Obviously whoever had taken the photos had been put up to it by that conniving woman, Ovelia Steinmetz. Then the image of another woman came into his mind. Prudence Howard. I gave that woman a list of the papers and magazines I advertise in. I'll murder her. That whore. But first he had to figure out a way to save his company.

Prudence Howard

Aruba

When I awoke the message light on the phone was blinking.

"Mr. Blackmore would like to meet for breakfast, downstairs on the Sunshine Terrace at 7:30."

What can he want? To apologize? I don't want or need his apology. I looked at the digital clock on the bedside table. 7:10. *Oh, god. He's probably on his way.*

I stood in the shower, and while the hot water ran over me, I knew I wanted to hear him out. I tried on three dresses before I decided on the red that accentuated my breasts. I don't usually do anything well before I've had my coffee, but here I was putting on just the right amount of mascara for the morning light.

Damn, I thought as I pulled the brush through my hair. It's not my fault Charles Blackmore has an idealistic view of life and relationships.

But as I applied the red lipstick that matched my dress, I became conscious of the fact that I rejected him out of hand because I was being prudent, as my mother hoped. Being dumped by Charles Blackmore would definitely be foolhardy.

Blackmore was at a table under an umbrella reading the *Morning Post*. He rose gripping his napkin as the maitre d' pulled out a seat for me, his eyes resting briefly on my cleavage. When he realized I'd noticed, he colored for an instant. I felt the heat of attraction that always passed between us, but I put my attention on the table that was laden with a thermos of coffee, freshly squeezed orange juice in a cooled jug, warm croissants under a napkin in a basket, and, a platter of crisp bacon.

"Thank goodness there's always a breeze. It's going to be hot," I said, as we both sat. *Why did you speak first? He'll think you've already forgiven him.*

Blackmore was nibbling on a rasher of the bacon.

"You did quite a job," I said, as I poured myself coffee. "The Europeans are going crazy." I took pleasure in noting that Blackmore's eyebrows contracted slightly. *Good, he felt the sting in my voice.*

"I had no idea it would hit the nerve it did. It looks like you and Ovelia were on the leading edge of a movement to protect animals in the wild." He bit into a buttered croissant. "Look...I wanted to meet with you... to assure you... that if Carlo makes any wrong assumptions about who set the media onto him, I'll straighten that out. I don't like to put other people in jeopardy. I won't let him blame you."

"Thank you, Charles." *So, he wants to look out for me. That's always a nice touch in a man.* I felt the old longing, the one where I love someone and he loves me back. I forced the feeling away. But, I did feel better about the Carlo thing. I believed Blackmore would confess before he'd let me take the fall.

I sipped the dark French roast and smiled at him. There was no point in staying angry. In a few days we'd be out of each other's lives forever. "Hopefully this media attention will get Carlo to stop the litigation rather than incite him to start another." I accepted the croissant Blackmore offered and broke it open.

"If Carlo's anything like me, he'll drop it and take care of his business. Lawsuits are a luxury few of us can afford. They waste a tremendous amount of time and energy."

He smiled back, but not with his eyes. *I guess he took my brush off seriously. He's not here to try to get me to change my mind about us.* I realized how disappointed I was.

I spread the melting butter and then laid my knife aside. "I agree. He should have just taken his lumps like a man. As far as I know, it's never been illegal to set up a business that's in competition with a former employer. But what upsets Ovelia and me is he's still killing the iguana." I could hear my voice rising, constricting with emotion. "Every time I think of those bloody skins… I'm no self-righteous vegan, Charles, I love a juicy steak, but at least we *raise* those animals." I was about to take a bite of the pastry but set it back on my plate. "Animals trying to make it in the wild. With shrinking habitats. It's hard enough for them already."

Blackmore's brow furrowed. "I thought the media attention would start small, just give him the jitters. Basically, get him to drop the case and see the error of his ways. Then I could call it off." He took a sip of coffee. "It's got a life of its own now, so I'd have a difficult, if not impossible time getting this to go away. I hope I haven't misjudged Carlo. He's very stubborn. He could be the sort of man who'll fight on, rather than have public opinion force him to quit. Got any ideas?"

"You might have avoided this problem if you'd asked me about your newspaper idea before you did it." That came out before I had a chance to edit.

"I deserved that. But, honestly Pru, it just might keep him off balance because he isn't sure who leaked the story."

Mollified by that piece of logic, I said, "Maybe it's best if the trial goes ahead. With public opinion on Ovelia's side, would a judge rule against her?" I picked up the croissant again and this time took a bite.

"Carlo hired the best lawyers, so I'd rather force him to quit. I don't like to leave decisions up to the arbitrariness of a judge's opinion. You never know what they'll do."

"What do you mean, 'arbitrariness'?" I asked.

"Spoken by someone who's never been sued."

"Not yet." I mentally knocked on wood.

"When you study the law as I've had to for my business, you soon realize that in most systems based on precedence, judges have a lot of leeway to interpret the law as they see it. I have come to believe the very act of trying to write a law down poses problems of meaning. That, in turn, means that the judge, using the law as he interprets it, rules based on his opinion."

"I see." I brushed a crumb from my lip. "You're a practical thinker, Charles. That's great, but my mother...her hobby was potting...taught me things aren't really finished until the glaze had been put on."

He looked at me quizzically.

"Glaze, you know, the hard coating of glass that makes the clay impermeable after it's baked."

Blackmore nodded.

"The problem is, Ovelia's still got feelings for him. It's the little bubble in the glaze that could ruin the pot. She could start to feel sorry for him. Maybe do something stupid like shut down her business. Women have been known to do things like that in the name of love. It would be great to think of a way to get Carlo to stop this crazy suit and close his factory before she has time to get too sentimental."

"You don't think Carlo returns her feelings, do you?" Blackmore asked.

"No I don't. He's never linked to anyone romantically. Always shows up in the society columns alone. He calls his yacht the *Angelita* as you probably know. It could be the name of the love of his life or something like that. Maybe an unrequited love or somebody died. I don't know, but I do think he'll never return Ovelia's feelings."

"You're right." Blackmore waited while the server removed his empty plate. "I'd never seen him with a woman until you showed up at his villa. Then, of course, I found out that was work." He blushed again.

What's with the blushing?

"I've found that cash, you know, a settlement, often works to put an end to things," Blackmore continued, "but Carlo's got too much money to think of settling. And he's way too angry." Blackmore poured us more coffee.

I began to think out loud. "Because he's king of a large shoe empire, a publicly traded empire, there are a lot of people with a vested interest in his success, right? The placard bearing and shoe-burning public will cause trouble for a while, but in a few months all will be well again. People love his shoes and most don't really care where the skins come from. The furor will die down. His investors won't bail permanently, will they?" I paused. "But then again, I don't know much about the stock market."

"I do. My company is public as well. It's never a good thing for your share price to fall. But if we really want to stop this guy...Wait. You've given me an idea."

"You wait, Charles. Could Carlo construe your idea as something else I could have done?" I said this with a smile and he smiled back. *He seems to be trying to make this right for Ovelia and me. Damn. I like him. This could have been good.*

"He did step over the line of decency," Blackmore said. "I don't like the slaughter of those reptiles any more than you do."

"What's this scheme you've concocted?"

He shook his head. "No. It'll be better if it's a surprise to everyone. Give me some time to get my idea in motion." He looked at his watch.

Of course it would be one of those slim gold watches that cost as much as this hotel. It nestled sensuously among the soft curly hairs on his arm.

"I don't mean to be rude, but if I'm to put this scheme into action, I have to make a few phone calls right now."

"Yes, right." I tried to read his face for some clue to what he was planning, but he was poker-faced. *You're infuriating. One minute I think you're an honourable guy and then you push my buttons by being such a Lone Ranger and I'm angry again.*

He stood up and placed some money under his plate. "Enjoy the rest of your breakfast." He looked out at the sea as if noticing it for the first time. "This *is* a really beautiful corner of the island."

He walked toward the restaurant entrance, moving elegantly across the warm sand, confidence oozing from every pore. As he disappeared into the building, I knew I'd made the biggest mistake of my life.

Charles Blackmore

Blackmore walked onto the hotel balcony and listened to the sea gently lapping on the beach. Tourists were lying under palapas and couples, holding hands, walked on the wet sand left by retreating waves. The air was hot but then a gust of wind cooled him.

"That damn woman," he muttered to himself. She said it wouldn't work and I don't have to be told twice. But he wondered why she'd worn that provocative dress. Immediately he conjured up the alluring scent of lavender and vanilla that had surrounded her. He reminded himself that anytime he'd let his guard down and started to fall for a woman, he'd regretted it. Fun was in accomplishment, money the yardstick. He could forget any woman by simply focusing on his work.

He walked back into his room and placed a call to his broker in London. "How many shares do I need to control Minelli Shoes?"

"I'll find out."

"Start buying it up. Now. There'll be some frenzied selling. Pick up everything you can. And let me know the minute I have control." By gaining control of Minelli Shoes, he would make a good deal of money when the stock returned to its former price.

Blackmore paced the length of the room. He knew Carlo no longer created all his shoe designs. For that he had a staff of talented young artists who had been inducted into the Minelli concept of shoe elegance and comfort. He simply approved their work, occasionally adjusting a drawing, except, of course, for the new technique he had been working on here in Aruba. But that was a small matter in the overall operation of Minelli Shoes. Carlo had expanded his empire to include valuable real estate, including entire shopping malls and office towers.

Blackmore pondered the possibility of running such a company. It was by buying up competitors that he had become the fourth largest container company in the world. He thought of his friendship with Carlo. But he reminded himself he hadn't made money by letting feelings for people get in his way. Running Carlo's design business *could* be perfect for a man who loved painting and anything connected to the world of art.

Blackmore sat on the sofa, ideas flickering through his mind. He made a call to his lawyer. "Find out if there are any laws in Aruba protecting the Green Iguana. Apparently, it's unique to this island."

Prudence Howard

After I finished breakfast, I took a taxi to Ovelia's house. The TV in the corner was tuned to the *BBC World News*. Ovelia muted it and looked up at me with eyes red-rimmed from crying. *This isn't good.*

"So you saw," I said, nodding towards the screen.

"Yes." She blew her nose and then said, "Would you like some coffee?"

This would be my third cup, but what the heck. The way the day was shaping up, I would probably need it. Ovelia's hand was shaking as she poured the steaming brew into a mug.

I have to do something to get her to stop. We're due in court in half an hour.

"He's scum. You know that Ovelia. He's ruthless and self-serving. His old world manners fooled me, too. I had a professor who said that all businessmen are evil. I was quite shocked by that statement at the time. 'All businessmen' was a pretty broad generalization. My *parents* owned a business. So, I walked up to him after the lecture was over and asked if he really meant *all* businessmen. He stopped for a moment to think, to see if that really fit into his worldview, I guess, and then said, 'yes.' I was so stunned by his answer I didn't think to ask why. But the statement stuck with me. In a way, I've been observing every businessperson I've come in contact with to see if that professor was right. Perhaps it's true that every *excessively* wealthy person has to have done something unethical in order to have earned so much money in *one* lifetime. It seems to me it's not in the natural order of things. We've been trained by our society to respect the wealthy, not to judge them. But maybe we *should* start to question how they make so much money. We've seen how Carlo does it."

"I know, but…and I know you don't want to hear this Pru…I think I'm still in love with him. What am I supposed to do about that? I feel like a schoolgirl. Talking about love when something so much more important is at stake. I really do know better than this."

"As unenlightened as I am in ways of the heart, I have a dim memory that when you're smitten, it's pretty much out of your control until the love object does something to really turn your heart off." I stirred sugar into my coffee and drank. "And the bastards always do something unforgivable, eventually." We smiled at each other. To my relief, she realized that I was trying to be funny.

"Thanks, Pru, I needed that." Her smile widened for a moment and then her face turned serious again. "But, Pru, Carlo's shown his bad side. Shouldn't I have seen enough damning evidence to destroy my feelings for him? After all, he's suing me. And he did cause the deaths of all those beautiful iguanas. A normal woman would have been repulsed. Instead, I keep thinking about how generous he was and not just with my salary. If my kids were sick or had something special at school, he always told me to take the time off. I remember how excited he'd get every time he found just the exact shoe color he wanted." Tears were forming in the corners of her eyes again. "What's wrong with me?"

"Like I said, he hasn't done 'the' thing yet. Your emotions are still winning over your logical mind. But while you're waiting, just keep reminding yourself he's been killing for money. It's not as if he were making cashmere sweaters from sheep that were merely shorn and could keep their lives. The guy was on his way to exterminating every last iguana on the island. But it looks like Blackmore's at least got his attention."

"I know, but will this ruin him? This reaction in Europe looks pretty bad."

"I, for one, don't care. I know that what I'm saying doesn't make a bit of difference to you right now, but as far as I'm concerned, he was the one who made the decision to murder the reptiles. If Blackmore hadn't kick-started this protest, eventually someone else would have discovered Carlo's sordid little secret and blown the whistle. There are a lot of people out there who care about wildlife. We had a reaction to Carlo's money-grubbing lust and so did all those women who've now destroyed their very expensive shoes. He crossed the line. His greed got the better of his judgment. He's slime."

"I know, I know."

But her voice wasn't convincing. It was time to leave so we got in her car and drove to the courthouse. At the public phone in the hallway, I made a call to Blackmore's hotel room. He wasn't in, so I left a detailed message explaining Ovelia's current state.

As I took my usual seat at the back of the courtroom, I wondered where the young man who had drawn angels for his mother had gone? Lost to the world forever, I supposed. The energy in the room was sluggish and heavy. Carlo's lawyer was standing, speaking to the judge. "Mr. Minelli is asking for time to return to Europe and curtail a very serious threat to his business interests. He has a duty to his shareholders."

Ovelia's lawyer jumped to his feet. "With all due respect, Mrs. Steinmez's business is considerably smaller that the plaintiff's and will be more seriously affected by any delay in the proceedings. My client is currently unable to get the bank loans she desperately needs to expand because of the Certificate of Pending Litigation Mr. Minelli placed on her personal assets and on her business. We submit that a delay will cause my client irreparable harm, while Minelli Shoes has a large professional staff to handle Mr. Minelli's interests."

I watched Ovelia repeatedly reach up and smooth her already tidy hair, wondering if her concern at this moment was more for Carlo than for her shoe business.

The judge's voice echoed harsh and cold off the wooden walls as he denied the adjournment. I wanted to jump up and kiss his graying temples.

Maybe the judge has seen the newspapers and he's hoping that if Minelli's company is really in that much trouble, if Minelli really has everything to lose, he'll drop the suit against Governor Steinmetz's daughter and stop slaughtering the iguana.

But I underestimated Carlo's unrelenting nature. Later that day, Blackmore returned my call. "Carlo told me that with time zone differences and telephone conferencing, he can talk with his executive team each morning before the trial begins. He'd prefer to handle it face to face in Italy, but he sensed the judge's dislike for him. Now Carlo feels he has even more reason to proceed. Apparently he works best when he feels his back is up against the wall. But don't worry, Pru. I have my other plan in the works. It'll crank up the pressure another notch."

So the trial continued, moving at the snail-like pace that the courts seem to need in order to determine guilt or innocence. I lost any patience I had left as I sat listening to the detailed, and in my view, irrelevant evidence. *Is it just my cynical side or do these lawyers speak so slowly because they get paid by the hour? It's enough to drive a normal person crazy.*

At the end of the second day of this torture, I got a call from Blackmore, suggesting Ovelia and I meet him at Tortelli's during the lunch recess. He had news.

The aroma of basil and garlic filling the restaurant reminded me I should visit Italy; always a relaxing thought.

Ovelia and I were led to a secluded booth where Blackmore sat, looking as fresh as usual.

How does he do that? As I slid onto the banquette, I felt like a bag of wet laundry, after only a short walk in the scorching sun.

Blackmore poured green-tinged wine into our glasses. "It's Vino Verde from Portugal," he said as he returned the bottle to the ice-filled bucket.

"I don't usually eat things that are green when they are supposed to be another colour. It reminds me too much of my student days when there were some really seriously offensive things in the back of my fridge," I said in an effort to get Ovelia to relax. The strain of the last two days showed on her face.

"Try it. I guarantee it won't be that nasty," Blackmore said.

I let the cool, crisp liquid fill my mouth, savouring the cleanness, so unlike the atmosphere in the courtroom.

"I suggest you file a counter-suit." Blackmore began.

Ovelia was nibbling absentmindedly on a breadstick, until the word counter-suit grabbed her attention. "Another lawsuit? Just what I don't need."

"It sounds daunting, I know. These legal entanglements can be the most frustrating of activities. But, sometimes, it is the only way to get your adversary's attention."

Ovelia put the breadstick on her side plate as if wondering how it happened to be in her hand. "On what grounds?"

"My lawyers found a Dutch law that just happens to apply here as well. It forbids the destruction of local flora and fauna for commercial purposes. Apparently it was put in place during the great tulip hysteria in the 1600's and has never been repealed. Carlo's lawyers must have missed it. Sometimes, guys who routinely succeed, get sloppy. Or if Carlo knows, maybe he thinks the rules don't apply to Minelli Shoes. But the bottom line is, Carlo asked you and the other staff to carry out an illegal activity."

"But we did it. Wouldn't we get in trouble, too?" Ovelia asked.

"The judge could be convinced there were mitigating circumstances. Besides, you quit the job when he wouldn't cease and desist." Blackmore paused. "There are never any guarantees in law, but by suing him for damages, saying that working for him irreparably harmed your reputation, you might...just *might* get him to drop this whole crazy thing. He is, after all, guilty of a crime."

The waiter came and took our food orders and Charles asked for another bottle of wine.

"But I'd be in the middle of another law suit," Ovelia said.

"Yes, but by putting pressure on him, you just might get him to close his operation and leave the island."

"If this law is brought to the attention of the courts, Charles, what would stop them from charging Carlo with the crime?" I asked.

"My guess is the local authorities would not prosecute him. International legal battles are not good for tourism. It tarnishes the image of an island that sells itself as peaceful and relaxing. And I *will* remind him he's getting a lot of pressure from his shareholders to get out of this situation. His share price is dropping."

"Really?" Ovelia said leaning forward. "Could this bankrupt him?"

"People are bailing."

"But, could he be ruined?" Ovelia repeated, her eyes wide.

Blackmore can surely see what I see. She's wavering.

The waiter placed steaming plates of pasta in front of us and offered freshly ground black pepper. I used the distraction to change the subject. " Ovelia, tell Charles about your ideas for growing the madder plant on the island." But she only mumbled a few words and began pushing food around on her plate. *Obviously that didn't work.*

Blackmore said, "Look, Ovelia, I know you were close to the guy. He's very charming. But now is the time to think of your children, of your new business, your staff. You can't afford the luxury of feeling sorry for him. We need the counter-suit if I'm going to be able to convince him he'd be better off dropping his case against you and returning to Italy to save his company."

Her face became distorted, but she forced back her emotions. "You'd do it if you were me, wouldn't you, Charles?" She took a large gulp of wine. "You're doing more for me then I'm doing for myself."

"You just set the suit in motion, and with your permission, I'll handle the rest."

Ovelia paused for a moment, considering. "I'll have to think about it."

Prudence Howard

Ovelia glanced at her watch as we walked out of the restaurant, now seemingly in control of herself. "My lease is ready to be signed. There's just enough time before we have to be back in court. Christian's an old friend. You'll like him. His offices are just down the street."

"You know me, I'm always interested in meeting a new man."

"He's very sweet. A contractor. Owns quite a few commercial buildings and he's currently building a hotel on the beach. Oh...and he's not married."

"Walk on, girl. What are we waiting for?"

We passed some tourists sporting Panama hats and licking ice cream cones of various colors.

"He knows about the lawsuit. He built Carlo's villa."

"It's a small, incestuous island you've got here."

"Yes, everyone knows everyone else's business, but that's part of the comfort. When things go wrong, people are there to lend a hand. Christian is letting me sign the lease without a damage deposit."

We walked down the palm-lined street in an easy silence, both of us so caught up in our own thoughts we ignored the clothes in the shop windows.

"Oh, I almost forgot. I'm supposed to call my agent before court resumes. Do you think your friend would let me make a call from his office?"

"Like I said, Christian's a very nice man. I'm sure he won't mind."

We were led into a modest second floor office with a commanding view of the harbour. Christian Dirksz thrust his large calloused hand at me as Ovelia introduced us. I guessed he was a hands-on guy. Not afraid to pick up a two-by-four.

"Please have a seat ladies," Christian sat down behind his desk. Files were arranged in an orderly fashion along the left side of the desk and his sharpened pencils, which had large green erasers attached to the ends, were lined up meticulously. *Not my type, just a bit too tidy.* He spoke in the clipped Dutch- accented English that usually put me on edge. But in spite of this, a warmth emanated from him.

"Could Prudence use your phone for a minute, Christian? She has an important call to the US."

"Certainly. Ovelia, why don't you and I go to the lunch room and bring back some coffee."

I dialed Sid Cosgrow's number.

"It's about time you got back to me. I've just finalized a book signing deal with Booktown. Five major cities and the option of more if all goes well. We're starting in Dallas in two days. Your hotels are all booked and I've looked after all the other flights, but you should arrange the flight from Aruba for sometime tomorrow. Just let me know your arrival time and I'll pick you up."

I've always liked the way Sid gets right to the point. He never wastes time on niceties. "Fantastic. I'll get on it."

There was a light knock on the door and Christian's head appeared. "My secretary said your call is finished."

"Yes."

As Ovelia laid the coffee cups out for each of us I sat back and studied the man, Christian. Unlike Ovelia he looked to be of pure Dutch descent, with light reddish-blond hair, cut short, emphasizing his angular head. His skin was pale even in this desert climate. He and Ovelia talked about her lease and he produced some papers that she signed.

Ovelia looked at her watch. "Oh, my goodness, I have to be back in the courtroom. Thanks, Christian for seeing me right away. Come on, Pru, let's go."

I thrust some money into his hands for the use of his phone, but he graciously refused. Out on the street I told Ovelia my news.

"I'm sorry I can't stay until the trial's over, but I'm just not famous enough yet to be telling these booksellers when and where I'll appear. I still need them more than they need me."

"I understand. I'm just so grateful you had time to be here at all. You've really helped me survive this."

"Let's hope Blackmore's scheme works and you'll be free of this thing soon."

Ovelia drove me to the travel agent after court adjourned. The only flight I could get at this late date left at mid-morning the next day.

Ovelia Steinmetz

Ovelia dropped Pru off at her hotel and then drove home. As she opened the front door she could hear the boys laughing in the kitchen. They'd be having a snack she guessed. But as she poked her head around the corner, they were sitting at the table with a pile of paper money between them. When they saw her they immediately stopped laughing and sat more upright, trying with all their collective might to look important.

"What's this? Where did you guys get this money?" she smiled back at them.

"We got a job. After school," the eldest, Robert, announced.

"A job. All three of you?"

"Yes. And we get paid every day. It's for you, Mom. We want to invest in your new business. We believe in you and, well, we've overheard you speak to Pru about how hard it is right now to get the money you need."

Ovelia thought her heart would melt, she felt such intense love for her children at that moment. How was it that she had managed to raise such thoughtful boys? She reached to each one and gave them a kiss on the top of the head. "Now, tell me, what is this job?"

"It's kind of gory, Mom." James replied. "It's a boys thing. You wouldn't want to do it."

Ovelia couldn't think what they could be doing. Washing cars? Raking leaves? But who would hire young boys to do that? "I can't guess. You'll just have to tell me."

"We set traps and catch those big green iguana that live all over the island. The gory part is that if they're not dead we have to kill them. We take along the garden shovel." Robert paused for a moment as if thinking whether or not that would be okay with his mother. "I hope that part is okay, Mom."

Ovelia felt like she had just been hit with the shovel. She sat down, her head dizzy. It had never occurred to her that her boys could be among the young kids who were put to work to get Carlo his inventory. She thought she was going to be sick. Then she saw her father looking at her in the way he did whenever she let him down. He never spoke in anger, but the look said everything, that she had disappointed him. He would be very disappointed to know that her boys were helping to exterminate Aruba's legacy.

"You aren't mad are you, Mom? James looked like he was about to cry. "We thought we were doing something good. But you're mad aren't you?"

Ovelia gathered herself together. "No, no. Not at all. You boys have been so very thoughtful. I'm just surprised, that's all. And we have to talk about killing the iguana."

Robert walked over to his mother, his shoulders squared. It's my fault, Mom. Some boys in my class were bragging about it and I wanted to be part of it. I...I didn't think about the killing part. We, all of us, just felt so grown up that we could get paid for doing something."

"I'm not angry with you. The truth is, I'm to blame. I've set a bad example by working for Mr. Minelli. But you know you have to stop, right?"

They huddled around her and she patted each one on the head. "We'll have to think of something good to do with this money. Let's all think about it for a few days. We can't possibly use the money for ourselves, now can we?"

They nodded.

"Now you guys run outside and play for awhile. I have a phone call to make before dinner."

Ovelia picked up the phone and dialed Charles' hotel. She knew that Carlo Minelli had just done *the* thing, as Pru said. "Hi, Charles. I've decided to go ahead with the countersuit." When she put the phone down she knew she'd lost all her romantic feelings for Carlo Minelli.

Charles Blackmore

Blackmore handed Carlo a copy of the Act of Parliament that made the Green Iguana a protected species in the Dutch Antilles. "You better read this. You could be in more trouble than you think. The penalties are quite severe, I'm told."

The two men were sitting on Carlo's veranda watching the sun set. The painter in Charles Blackmore savoured the deep purple fingers of the palm fronds that complemented the orange rays of light reflecting off the water. He poured more tonic water into the icy glass.

Carlo's brow furrowed and he shouted, "What's the meaning of this? Why did you bring this to me? I'm not being charged with this crime. In fact," he blustered, the veins on his neck and forehead standing out like small cords, "I didn't know this law existed."

"It seems the Dutch put it into law at the time of the great Tulip Bubble in the 17th century. It's vague, but it includes flora and fauna. Anyone could potentially bring this information to the crown prosecutor. Frankly, I don't know why your lawyers didn't inform you about it before you got into business here. They seem to have been asleep at the switch." Blackmore was pleased to see this revelation excited the Italian, believing people always made mistakes when they got excited. He also knew Carlo would be even more distressed if he knew that he, Blackmore, had invented a law that did not, in fact, exist.

"The talk on the street, Carlo, is that if you continue with the case against Ovelia, you'll be charged. She's a local. Didn't you take that into account when you started this action?"

Carlo's face darkened. "What exactly have you heard?"

"She's well liked. This is her home turf."

Carlo scowled. "What do you think I should do?"

"You could save your ass by dropping the charges. Say you've had it with Aruba. That you'll never do business here again. You have to get out to protect your shareholders. You know, blah, blah, blah. Whatever you have to say to get out of Dodge."

"Out of Dodge?"

"It's an old expression from the westerns I watched when I was a kid. It means to leave this lovely rock."

"You think I should drop the case? Would you?"

"I would. Few fortunes are made or saved by standing on principle. You know that. Business is a pragmatic affair. We, people like you and I, didn't get rich by letting it get personal.

"The way I look at it, you can't win and you'll look like an ogre trying. You need to get your business back on track or you could end up losing the whole thing. And for what? An employee who called you on something you shouldn't have been doing in the first place. Give her this victory. It's small potatoes. You have much more to lose if you don't go home and clean up this mess."

Carlo stood and paced up and down. "You know my atelier is everything to me."

"Yes, I do. You set it up to honour Angelita, correct?"

"Every day, I think of her." He ran his hand over his balding head. "We were children. In the bloom of love. A love more than love. Her soft breath on my neck each night as we lay together. My angel."

Carlo's face returned to its normal olive shade. He sat back down just as the sun disappeared below the western horizon; the only light now was from the amber colored lights in Carlo's study, drifting out onto the veranda. "The stars...when they come out in the night sky...my Angelita, is there. She and I together. I commune with her. She moves through the night sky like a sigh. I barely hear her, but I feel her breath caress my cheek. And then I remember the fragrance of her silken hair rinsed in lemon water.

"It was such a long time ago, but she is as fresh and beautiful in my memory as the last day I saw her. It would destroy me if the business were forced into bankruptcy. With the atelier creating shoes in her memory, she stays alive."

"As I told you before, I envy you. You have had a greater love than most people would even hope to experience. But, well," Charles sat up straighter, "isn't love supposed to spread its goodness around? Was she the sort of woman who would have killed the iguana for a fashion statement?" He was taking a chance, but it was time to see what Carlo's ethics really were.

The wind was up now, rustling through the palms. Carlo's maid came out to turn on the outdoor heaters. Blackmore was impressed how Carlo's staff anticipated his every need.

Carlo looked thoughtful, perhaps even a little ashamed of himself. "I will consider your point."

"Look, Carlo. I'm going back to my hotel. You'll probably want to discuss things with your lawyer before tomorrow's proceedings."

Both men stood. Carlo clasped Blackmore's hand. "I appreciate your letting me know what you've heard. You've been a true friend. I know you're caught in the middle. Miss Steinmetz is a friend also. You are a man of character, Charles. I won't forget this."

"I'd like to see everyone win. If that's possible."

"I know, my friend."

Blackmore led the way through the study, thinking of the shares of Minelli Shoes he now owned. Carlo would have a much different view of their friendship if he were aware of that fact.

Carlo Minelli

In the morning as his driver maneuvered the Mercedes away from the villa, Carlo was still pondering Blackmore's recommendation. From his attaché case he took out a memo he'd just received from his chief financial officer in Milan. "Someone is buying up all your shares as the price is falling. This could be a hostile takeover, perhaps a competitor who wants to destroy us. Whoever it is, now owns close to the twenty-seven per cent required for control. You are urgently needed here, Carlo. As you know, many of your employees have invested heavily in the stock. It could ruin many families if things go badly."

Carlo put the page back into the case. Years ago, when he had needed capital to expand he'd reluctantly gone public. He knew any number of fashion houses could take advantage of this crisis. His was a cutthroat business, designs kept locked in safes until shown on runways in Milan.

He watched the rows of palms slip by as they approached the traffic circle leading past Blackmore Shipping. The man was right. He had been a fool to get into this fight over such a trifling matter.

In the conference room at the courthouse where they met each day to discuss the case, his lawyer, Maxim, was waiting. “Miss Steinmetz has started a counter-suit.”

Carlo felt as though a huge weight had just been dropped on him from a vast height. “What? On what grounds?”

“That you had your employees commit a crime. The documents state it is illegal to kill the Green Iguana. They’re a protected species only found here. You need to get her to drop these charges, Carlo. It could be serious.”

Carlo glowered at the man. “If I didn’t have such fools for lawyers, I wouldn’t be in this mess.” If only Charles had told me of this law earlier, I could have dropped the case before she acted. Carlo stood, running his hand over his balding head. His mind was racing. “I know what I need to do. Just leave it to me.”

The two men walked into the hallway. Ovelia and Prudence were sitting on the wooden benches outside the courtroom door, talking. Carlo looked at his watch. He had just enough time before the session began to execute his plan. As he walked toward the women, he noted Charles Blackmore was approaching from the far end of the hallway.

Carlo stopped in front of Ovelia and took her hand in his. He saw the alarmed look on Prudence Howard’s face, just as he had hoped.

“Ovelia, I’ve made a terrible mistake. I was angry with you for criticizing me. I have always had a great respect for you. I wanted you to respect me, too. When you left my employ, I took it personally. Very, very personally.”

Ovelia was silent.

"I have feelings for you, I didn't realize I had. I reacted so negatively because I was hurt." He opened his hands to her in a pleading gesture.

"Hurt?" Ovelia managed to squeak out the word.

"Yes, I care a great deal for you and to prove it, I'm going to withdraw my suit. The fact of the matter is I'm very proud of you, the way you got your business going. I know you didn't steal designs from me. Your shoes are fresh, interesting and definitely your own. The truth is, I was upset you were able to do it all without my help."

Carlo looked at Prudence Howard. He could see she didn't believe one word of what he said. She loathed him. He felt the searing heat of her gaze as she glared at him, tight lipped. But when he looked back into Ovelia's eyes, they were teary, and that was all that mattered.

"Maxim, kindly arrange to meet with the judge," Carlo said, as he turned back to Ovelia, looking deeply into her eyes. "Tell him we are withdrawing the suit."

The lawyer turned to do as he was commanded and walked down the hallway.

"I have decided to close my factory here, Ovelia. I will not be responsible for the destruction of any more Green Iguana."

Prudence stood and moved towards the exit. "Listen, Carlo. I don't know what you're up to, but you better be serious about this."

Ovelia turned to Prudence, her face hot with emotion. "Why wouldn't he be serious? You're so suspicious."

"It's just my novelist's mind. Always looking for the motive that moves the plot along." *Now I'm the bad guy...*

has she forgotten this is the man who killed thousands of her precious iguana? How can she even begin to trust what he says?

Ovelia put her tear stained face on Carlo's shoulder and he began caressing her.

Prudence glanced at her watch. "Ovelia, looks like a happy ending. You two just have to complete the paperwork. Meanwhile, I have to get to the airport." She pulled up the handle of her suitcase and walked out of the building.

Charles Blackmore

London, England

It was another overcast day in London, the mist coming in at intervals then turning to rain that pelted onto the street below. But here in Charles Blackmore's office, lamps strategically placed around the room glowed a soft yellow, countering the somber mood of the day. He sat at his Edwardian desk with its dark green blotter, feeling connected to the expansive English countryside as he ran his hand along the antique's smooth walnut surface.

Blackmore forced himself to think of work, the deal with the Mongolians he had just completed. Memories of riding a camel – sleeping in a yurt flashed across his mind. He enjoyed the Mongols' wry sense of humor. They had become friends and, as a result, his name, written on the side of his containers, would soon be appearing in the capital. Had he taken advantage of their seeming naivety? No, he was sure that they'd had the best of him. They were skilled at negotiating and bartering with foreigners, a practice that had allowed them to survive for centuries as nomads inhabiting vast areas of land too poor to grow crops. They thrived by following domesticated animals across vast pastures, owning only what they could easily transport. These customs revealed an intense understanding of the land and environment.

Usually achieving a goal made Blackmore content, but that wasn't the case today. He realized that simply increasing his wealth was no longer enough. He looked at the contract in front of him. It represented a good deal of work, hard negotiating. He wondered if it was the nature of human beings to never feel truly satisfied.

He got up and poured a coffee from the thermos on his credenza. He was longing to see Prudence Howard. Continually forcing down his desire had become tiresome, making his days an agony. He had lost the power to forbid his feelings. Her face would come unbidden and refuse to go away. If he possessed her, he wondered, would he be happy at last.

He thought of one of the last times they were together. She'd worn a provocative dress, even though she'd told him a relationship would never work. He wondered how she could know that when he hadn't so much as kissed her. Why was he always attracted to the ones who didn't want him?

Blackmore sat back at his desk and repeatedly clicked his pen open and shut. He remembered her book, her angst about the loss of the black rhino. Perhaps she's just more passionate about saving animals than being with a man. That possibility was depressing.

The rain started again. He watched people streaming by on the sidewalk below, their umbrellas reflecting the light from the street lamps into his office. Blackmore pondered the news he'd received a few days before from his manager in Aruba. Ovelia Steinmetz had secured a deal with a shoe distributor in Miami and needed to ship the product. He shook his head, thinking about the temerity of both women, respecting both of them.

He picked up the phone. He didn't want to be alone again for dinner. But as he waited for it to be answered, he sighed and hung up. That damn woman, he thought. I can't have her and I can't go back to my former way of life either.

Prudence Howard

Sun Valley Writers' Conference, Idaho, 1986

As I flew over the Sawtooth Range in southern Idaho, I was thankful that the two weeks of book signings were almost at an end. Hundreds more books had been sold, but I was tired. There was just this writers' conference to attend and I could have a break. What I remembered from having attended these events was that people asked simple questions like, how did you get your idea for your book, were the characters modeled after anyone you know, things like that. So I was sure the morning would flow smoothly. But Sid Cosgrow's warning that my book was quite political and there could be some backlash came into my mind. I brushed the thought away as I exited the small plane and walked across the tarmac to the terminal, where a limo was waiting to drive me to the hotel in Sun Valley.

When we drove through the town of Ketchum, I was instantly taken with it. *It's so different from Whistler. It looks like this was an actual ranching community at one time: old authentic buildings, and a great little clapboard church. Oh, there's a sign on it. It's an Italian restaurant now.*

In my room, I threw myself on the bed and took in the view of the mountain. Pretty. But compared to the high peaks of Whistler, it seemed like a hill.

There was enough time to have a short nap before the dinner that Marjorie Sennet, the event coordinator, had arranged so that all the authors could meet. The program indicated I was to be the last speaker in the morning session.

In the brightly lit conference room the next morning I tried to listen attentively to the answers given by the other participants, but the questions were so general, so unbelievably inane to my way of thinking that my mind wandered to the meetings I'd had with Sid Cosgrow in L.A.

We'd had dinner with the Book-of-the-Month Club executive; mine was to be the selected monthly book. The next morning Sid and I met in the Beverly Hills Hotel breakfast room. As usual my plate was piled high with watermelon, pineapple, green grapes, and sliced bananas. I remembered pulling the silvery tab off the plastic yoghurt container and spooning it over the fruit. We discussed the details of the proposed agreement.

I have Ovelia to thank for all this, I thought. 'Why don't you write what you are passionate about?' And that was the turning point.

"Your book is really selling well," Sid said. "You've hit some kind of nerve with people who care about endangered animals, but there is one thing that I'm concerned about when you're at the conference in Idaho. You've given your characters some strident political opinions about why the world is the way it is: greed, power, selfishness. Over population. It's part of the reason for the great sales figures, but there could be some backlash."

I swallowed the pineapple I'd been chewing. "I can always return to Canada. No one would think of looking for a political radical there, now would they?"

Sid looked across the table and smiled. He had a stack of pancakes on his plate smothered in thick, gooey syrup. I smiled back, thinking how much his round shape echoed his food choices. "But you have to admit, Sid, there are too damn many people on this planet and that's what's causing all the problems. There wouldn't be all these issues if there were fewer of us. The population has expanded from two billion after World War Two to five billion today. Everybody's life style is improving at the expense of Nature."

"I know, Pru." He stopped to place a piece of pancake running with syrup into his mouth. He chewed and swallowed. "But," he said as he wiped his lips with his napkin, "just be careful how you answer the questions. You're there to sell books, not to fight for your causes. Let your book do that."

I knew I should listen to him. He'd been in the writing game a long time, supporting new and rising stars, but here in this corner table we were unlikely to be overheard and I wanted to rant. "Animals have just as much right to be here as people, but people ignore that fact, big time. I just don't understand why we humans feel ourselves superior to other creatures. Why is saving a human life so much more important than saving grizzly bears?"

Sid's eyes popped wide open. "That's exactly what I mean. You can't say that at the conference."

"I know." I gave him a wry smile. "It's just us and I need to get this off my chest. People might not be the best thing that happened to the planet. I think it was Mark Twain who said that evolution had made a mistake when humans came along. Don't get me wrong, I wouldn't wish that anyone alive now was dead, but I think the Chinese have it right with the one child policy. Believe me, with all our technological advances, a smaller number of humans could live very well on this planet without doing the harm we're now doing."

Sid slid his knife through the pancakes and lifted his fork again to his lips. I had to admit that he made his food look delicious, even though it was a carbohydrate overload.

"I agree with you there, Pru. I can't think of one advantage in such a large population except, of course, it fuels economies. But take California, for instance. My grandfather settled here in the 1920's. He used to tell me about the acres of orange groves and large horse ranches that graced this valley. Now it's wall-to-wall houses."

I signaled to the waitress that we needed more coffee. "What is the matter with the human race, Sid?"

Sid pushed his plate away and took a sip of coffee. "We've done great things, too. Don't forget that. Advances in medicine, for instance. The signing of the Civil Rights Act by President Johnson in 1964."

"I just don't get it, though. As far as we know, amoeba and protozoa don't think about the past or ponder the future. Humans have the ability to reflect on their actions. With more people, the mystical concept of a shared consciousness should be making more of us wise. But we don't act like we are," I said as I ate another spoonful of pineapple and yoghurt.

"I accept that you are passionate about this, Pru. But if you say this stuff at the conference, make sure you have that airline ticket to Canada in your pocket."

I heard my name being called on the sound system. The person standing in front of the microphone was staring at me waiting for a response and I hadn't heard the question. I could feel myself blush and hoped the thick make-up I was wearing would conceal it from the audience. "I'm sorry. I was thinking about the last response and wasn't listening. Could you please repeat your question?"

"I asked if you are a vegetarian and if that influenced your writing? I mean, you seem very upset that animals are killed. This is ranching country. We've pretty sensitive about that in these parts."

I thought back to the rolling hills I had driven through yesterday, how I liked the town. "I love a great steak, believe me. No, my only problem is the killing of animals for the trophy value. I realize the work that you ranchers do to keep your herds. I only wish we were doing that in Africa where the black rhino is killed for the horns, not the meat." I thought about my answer and then added, "well we shouldn't kill them for meat either, but with the overcrowding in Africa, they do that sometimes as well." I could hear Sid's words cautioning me, but it was too late, I'd said them.

"Thank you for clarifying that," the questioner said, straightening the cowboy hat on her head. "I'll fix you a steak anytime you come by."

The next speaker had moved to the microphone. "Do you think you were telling the truth about the problems in the world when you wrote your novel?"

The truth. That's at least a meatier question, but she looks angry. I better just answer her simply and then I'm out of here. "Look, I don't know about the truth. In fact, I doubt that there is anything like a higher truth that we could all come to agree on. When I wrote this book, I looked at some situations in the world that I thought could be made better in some way and then I proceeded to make up a story where my characters lived in those situations. I tried to see if I could make any sense out of the problem that black rhinos are being slaughtered for their horns, that the rhino itself as a species is disappearing, and that that could cause harm to the web of life. But maybe I'm wrong. I certainly don't claim to hold any magic lantern that illuminates the truth. I can only hope that my book gets people thinking."

"Your protagonist says there are too many people in the world and that is the reason the animals are being killed."

"Yes, that's correct."

"What makes you think there are too many people in the world?"

"Well, I think it is important to separate my thoughts from those of the character I created. I have personal political views, but they are not necessarily the same as those of a character I invent."

"But you must have those thoughts or you couldn't write about them."

"I don't think that is true..."

Another woman in the audience stood up. "I have five children. Are you trying to tell me that I shouldn't have?" The woman's face was distorted with anger.

"Look, I came here to discuss my book, to explain, if at all possible, the methods I use during the creative process..."

"Well, I don't think you could have written this book with such passion if you don't yourself believe it," the same woman continued.

I could feel myself flush with anger and I swallowed hard in order to slow down my response, but I felt a surge of adrenalin. This woman was starting to piss me off. "If you really want to know my personal view I'll tell you. I read somewhere, maybe the Willy Brandt report concerning world hunger, that people in third world countries have lots of children because they don't have a social safety net to provide for them in their old age. At the same time, the developed world uses four-fifths of the world's resources. I made the mental leap that children added in the first world take resources from those in the third world. It doesn't seem right to me that all sorts of people go to bed hungry every night while others live their lives surrounded by every luxury, most of which they don't really need."

"So you have a problem with rich people. You must have made a good deal of money from the massive sales of your book."

I looked over at Marjorie who was about to stand up, but I motioned for her to stay seated. Something in me wanted to answer this question. Had I deliberately made the novel political? Had I used my art to try to serve some purpose other than to entertain? It was true that the book was selling inordinately well. I had thought it was because it was well written, but maybe, just maybe, it was the message that people were after. Except for these two women, who seemed to be quite triggered by my opinions in the book.

"No, I don't have a problem with 'rich people' as you put it. I do have a problem with how some people make their money. People like Bentley Tyler in my novel."

"Yes, just like you believe I had too many children."

"Honestly, I don't understand why this is such an issue for you. It's just one point of view. *Boy, you silly bitch. You wouldn't be so upset about this if you weren't feeling guilty.*

Well you asked for it lady, I will speak my mind. We base our whole economic system on growth, and that requires more consumers all the time. I think our most pressing problems would go away if, given the current state of technology to support our standard of living and that standard spreading across the globe, we stopped reproducing at such a fantastic rate. And last time I checked, you Americans allow freedom of speech in this country. Look, I took a point of view about this and wrote a novel about it. And I did want to write something that was credible."

"Credible?" The questioner's terse voice clawed through the microphone, her hands were working the edges of a long scarf she had tied loosely about her neck.

"Credibility requires only that something *look* believable. Hemingway said something about that. That you had to write the truth. Well, how does one do that? His answer was that you had to write things that *could* be true. I spend time contemplating things. I don't *know* that I'm correct in my assessment. But, that's why I write."

I nodded at Marjorie to get up now. A forced smile parted her thin lips as she spoke into her microphone. "As much as this is a fascinating discussion, we have run out of time. I want to thank you all for attending."

Did I actually just say that I don't have a problem with rich people? Some, like Carlo Minelli, certainly let their ego get the better of them. I see now that others, like Charles Blackmore, can simply be at the right place at the right time and with hard work, wealth comes their way. I can't bring myself to call him evil. In fact, he's actually a very caring guy.

Prudence Howard

Vancouver, BC, July 1986

I landed at Vancouver Airport on a sweltering afternoon, jumped into a yellow cab and directed the Sikh driver to take me to Ye Old English Fish and Chip Shoppe on Denman Street.

"How's it going this summer? Is Vancouver busy?"

"Yes, Miss. Very busy. We are hosting the Expo 86. Did you not know?"

The cabbie eyed me through the rearview mirror. He must have been wondering what planet I'd dropped in from. I'd been so involved with writing, book signings and the events in Aruba that I'd completely forgotten about the world's fair, but it did explain my difficulty obtaining an airline ticket. I smiled as sweetly as I could at the driver so he would believe I was sane, then settled back to soak in the atmosphere of my hometown.

Nothing appeared to have changed as we drove up Granville Street. All my favorite shops were still there. We crossed False Creek then looped around to Denman and stopped across from the fish and chip place that my dad now called home. I grabbed my bag, handed the driver the fare and a tip and stood looking across the street to the small restaurant.

He'd written that he'd married again. Rita was her name. She owned the shop and the two floors of apartments above. It was an old building with white plastered walls and dark angled beams. Large plate glass windows were dressed up to look like the mullioned windows of Tudor times.

The shop door opened. My dad rushed out, running across the busy street and sweeping me up in a giant bear hug.

"How's my girl?" he crooned into my ear. "Let me get a look at a world famous author." He dropped me to the ground and stood back, looking me up and down. "You're even more beautiful than I remembered."

One thing about my dad is he thinks the world of me, even if no one else does or should. I'm his girl and wonderful in his eyes. I ate it up.

"Rita's dying to meet you." Dad picked up my bag and we ran across to the restaurant. Inside was quiet. Not many people eat fish and chips at four in the afternoon.

Rita, a matronly British woman in her mid-fifties came out from behind the cash register desk, straightening the frilly apron she wore over a printed pastel Marks and Spencer dress. She gave me a close, friendly hug. "Welcome home," she said. "And I mean that. You are to consider this your home whenever you're in Vancouver. And...you can stay as long as you like. One of the apartments was vacated just after you wrote to say you were coming. It's on the floor above and looks out to the street. We figured a writer would need to look at the locals. Get ideas for characters," she smiled at me with real warmth. I was moved by her acceptance of me, sight unseen. It spoke to me of her love for my dad.

She looked lovingly at him and he put an arm around both of us.

"Come on, Pru. Let's have a coffee and you can tell us all about your adventures," Dad said. "We'll take your bag up later and get you settled in."

Rita scurried to the side bar and poured coffee from a chrome thermos. British flags hung everywhere and small wall brackets held old English souvenirs: china mugs, bulldog ornaments, pictures of Britain during the earlier part of the century, and plates with pictures of the royal family. The tables were covered with red plastic cloths so that a quick wipe would make the table ready for the next hungry guest.

"This place was my saving grace when my first husband, Henry, died," Rita said. "It kept the wolf from the door and got me over the sadness. No one wants to see a mourning woman serving them beer and chips."

"It looks like you've been very good for my dad, Rita," I said, taking a sip of the coffee. I turned to my father. "How did you meet this wonderful woman?"

"After your moth...I mean, after you left, I looked for a job. With the build-up to Expo, there was work everywhere. I became a bellman at the hotel across the street, but finding a room was a lot harder. I kept answering ads and was getting really depressed by the squalor of anything I could afford. It's amazing what some landlords try to rent. I decided I'd better get a job moonlighting so I could afford to pay more. A few days later I noticed an ad in Rita's window. She was looking for a barman. Rita hired me then and there." My dad reached out and touched my hand. "I know what you're thinking. But I wasn't tempted to drink."

Rita got up to settle the bill for a departing client.

"She's such a simple, hardworking, woman. Mothers all the customers and they just love her. I fell for her, too. I'd never do anything to hurt her. She's my princess...after you, of course." Dad ruffled my hair, something that had always irritated me as a kid, but I adored it today. "She married me even though I had nothing but my hard work and love to contribute."

"Rita doesn't seem to mind." I looked over at her. She was talking and laughing with the man who was leaving. I envied my dad at that moment. Sure, I now had a fair bit of money to show for my years away, but no lasting love. Charles Blackmore's face flashed across my mind.

Over the next few weeks I settled into writing. The tiny, one-bedroom apartment had wooden window frames and crown molding that wrapped around the high-ceilinged walls. Everything was painted white with the exception of natural fir floors that glowed from years of being waxed. I bought a comfy white sofa, some lamps and a dark burgundy table I placed at the window that faced down onto Denman Street. There I ate and wrote, the days and weeks merging so I couldn't tell them apart.

Rita was right about the view of the street. From my perch, I could observe the comings and goings of everyone, undetected. One morning I watched an elderly Italian, with a great drooping mustache, go into the shoe repair shop across the street. He was carrying a paper bag that probably held a pair of dilapidated shoes. I let my mind wander as I made up the story of his life. He became a sad widower who, in order to make a living, rented rooms to students and one day was killed by a drug-crazed adolescent, much to the horror of his tenants. Another day, a gay couple who dared to walk openly hand in hand, became a famous opera duo who were allowed their eccentric ways by adoring fans. There they were, new characters, new plots for the choosing. I wrote while the royalty cheques kept coming in.

One Thursday, I put on my sneakers and running shorts and headed to Stanley Park where, set against the dark green firs and cedars, all the deciduous trees were turning bright red, yellow and orange. A light dusting of snow had fallen on the tops of the North-shore mountains, emphasizing the famous lions that slept there in granite. The sea wall was crowded with walkers, kids on roller blades, and cyclists out to catch the last rays of summer.

After a month of running every other day, I was surprised that I could still only make it about three miles before I had to rest. If I kept going, a horrible stitch would catch in my side, nearly doubling me over. All those bottles of good French wine and hours of writing at a desk had taken their toll.

At the mermaid statue I stopped to catch my breath and looked toward the Lions Gate Bridge. Marine traffic was moving under it from both directions. One large ship heading into Coal Harbour had blazoned across the side, "Blackmore Shipping." My heart lurched. I hadn't thought of Charles Blackmore for weeks. Well, that wasn't exactly true. I hadn't thought of him on purpose, but he came to me at all times of the day and night. That face, the touch of his hand, the assured way he did things.

Clouds raced across the sky as the wind rose; so to keep my muscles from seizing up, I made myself put one foot in front of the other. In my head I could hear Mick Jagger's raw voice chanting, "You can't always get what you want. You can't always get what you want." Then, "But if you try sometimes, you just might find you get what you need." I have always loved that lyric, but now it seemed to have a more intense meaning. I had *wanted* Blackmore, but what I *needed* was success as a writer. So I could 'pay my own way', as my dad always said. But, if I got what I needed why wasn't I truly satisfied?

I rounded the last corner of my run. The endorphins had kicked in a while back and there was no more pain with my breath, just smooth, effortless running. As I turned back onto Denman Street, I slowed to a walk. Upstairs in my apartment I sat on the floor and did my stretches, took a quick shower, and then went to the kitchen to pour a glass of pinot. I sank into the down cushions of my sofa and put my feet up on the coffee table. Opening my dog-eared copy of Aristotle, I tried to find what he had said about need and want. Somewhere I had underlined a passage about the tendencies inherent in all things to seek a natural fulfillment.

Here it is, "Each thing seeks its own perfection" and further on "that Nature does nothing in vain." I lay my head back and closed my eyes letting those thoughts run through my mind. *I guess that's what I've done. My own perfection was to become a writer and I've done that. I've made money, serious money. Enough money to be secure for a lot of years, with some left over to keep me from being bored.*

I took a sip of wine and swished it about in my mouth, then swallowed, the sharpness of the good pinot lingering. It's natural for a vine to find its perfection in producing a fully matured grape. So if I was now completely fulfilled, had achieved what I needed, why was I thinking of, or more truthfully, longing for Charles Blackmore? Then there was this surprising question: Do I *need* him?

My problem is I don't like the idea of needing someone. It sounds so, well...*needy.* I know how to work hard at my craft. I can discipline myself to sit at the computer every day, and turn out page after page of work. But to seek love from another person, the kind of love that Rita and my father have found...now that's a scary thought. If you let yourself really get into someone and they don't want you back...that leads to real heartache. And who needs that?

I drained my glass and returned to the kitchen, deciding to grill a steak for dinner. Want or need? Want or need? The question kept going through my head as I watched the butter begin to smoke in the cast iron frying pan. The answer was that I did want Charles Blackmore, but was he something that I actually needed in order to fulfill myself?

I placed the steak into the hot pan and heard it sizzle. Was Blackmore the sizzle or the steak?

I had started to date: a lawyer who lived around the corner and often ate in the restaurant, as well as a guy I met in my Tai Chi class. He was a local film director who was a bit eccentric, but nice. They both seemed second rate compared to Blackmore. I didn't even have the desire to sleep with those guys - - me, who really likes sex. What was my body trying to tell me about need and want?

I turned the steak over in the pan, letting the overhead fan draw up all the steam. The truth was I hadn't heard a word from Charles Blackmore, the man who said he was interested in me. Give your head a shake, Pru. You know there is still that tiny little problem that you told him it wouldn't work. You know he wouldn't want you when he learned you'd been living off those men in Europe.

I cut into the steak to see how pink it was in the middle. *His memory will fade and I will fall for some nice mechanic who will make my life full of love.* At least that was the plan.

A few days later, I was sitting at my table finishing up the reconciliation of my bank statement, shocked at how my savings account was growing. It was a hot, late autumn day and I wanted to stretch my legs, so I got ready for a run. As was my habit I went into the restaurant to let Dad and Rita know where I was going. They were sitting across from some customers who had become friends and I overheard the other man say that this was a really great operation the two of them had. I saw my dad wince in pain. It was momentary; I'm sure the other couple would not have noticed, but I noticed. My dad's comment that he had nothing to offer financially had stayed with me even though it seemed to make no difference to his new wife. But I understood he was going against his dictum – you have to pay your way – and he was suffering. Then I knew what I would do with that money in my bank account.

Dad was skeptical at first, but then I convinced him it was my way of 'paying *my* way' for all he'd done to raise me. I wanted to give him the money, but he would only agree to a loan, with everything done in writing and signed in front of a notary.

That night Rita and I were having dinner at her table in the restaurant kitchen. It was amazing to me how she could relax while she kept an eye on everything that went on with her staff and customers. Nothing seemed to fluster the woman.

"Rita, I have a proposition."

"Well, that sounds serious, dearie."

"My dad and I want to buy into your business. Forty-nine per cent. That way you still have control, but it would free up some cash for you."

Rita's eyes narrowed. "You father doesn't have any money." She fidgeted in her seat.

This was the first time I'd ever seen her look uncomfortable when talking about my father. It dawned on me that she suspected he had been lying to her. "Actually, I won't be part of the partnership, just my dad. I've been thinking of a way to invest some of my book royalties and dad has agreed to borrow the money from me, at a very fair interest rate. I mean if the idea appeals to you."

I saw her muscles relax a bit but she still wasn't convinced.

"You know. You two could take a nice long trip back to England. Show my dad where you grew up. I can manage things while you're away. I'm sure my dad told you about our hotel in Whistler. I did every job in the place." I dipped a piece of fish into the tartar sauce. "What do you say?"

Rita looked dazed, but slowly I could see her eyes light up as my idea began to take form. I hoped she could see that I was attempting to save face for my father. They would own the place together and have some time to enjoy each other. It was my gift to this woman who loved the only man in the world who knew me and loved me anyway.

"I don't see how I can refuse," Rita said, tears forming in her eyes. "You really are a wonderful daughter, just as your dad has always said."

We signed all the papers and they were leaving for a month as soon as Expo ended. I suggested they should stay away longer, but Rita said even though she trusted me to run things perfectly, she just didn't think she could. Frankly, I was relieved. Even though with the Fair closed business would be less hectic, I wasn't sure I was up to looking after the place for much longer than that.

Charles Blackmore

London

Charles Blackmore decided that the quickest and easiest way to forget about Prudence Howard was to force himself to resume his way of life, the one that had worked so well before he met her.

That evening after a dinner at the Roof in the Kensington Garden Hotel, he took the flamboyant red head, Adele, to a hotel room he'd booked. Blackmore never brought women to his home. The one time he'd done that he'd seen the girl's eyes widen as she took in his art collection, and his very expensive custom made furnishings. The less they knew about him the better.

Adele stood with drink in hand on the thick carpeting. Blackmore put his glass on the bedside table and clasped the pull on the closure that went from her neck to below her waist. Giving a gentle pull, the dress began to slip open. It had a built in bra, so when he slid it from her shoulders, two perfectly formed breasts with erect pink nipples presented themselves.

Usually this slow, methodical way of undressing a woman was enough to arouse Blackmore, to create a sense of urgency that enhanced the evenings of lust, but that purposely remained devoid of any tender emotion. As he slid the dress further, to uncover gently rounded hips, the image of Prudence Howard entered his mind, walking up from the beach in front of Carlo's villa, naked. He remembered how the sight of her body had jolted him. The woman now standing patiently in front of him, paled in comparison. His desire for her evaporated.

Blackmore coughed and turned away, retrieving the envelope of money from the top of the dresser. "Sorry, but this isn't going to work out for me tonight."

She was shocked and covered her breasts with trembling hands. He did feel sorry for her. Quite likely, no other client had sent her away at this moment in the procedure. Procedure, Blackmore thought. That's what this has become for me.

The next day before dawn, Blackmore drove out of London to Lord Pembroke's estate.

Prudence Howard

Vancouver

A few days before Dad and Rita were to leave, I was at my table, working on a new story that included the Italian I'd seen walking into the shoe repair shop across the street. Ignoring the odor of car exhaust that wafted up from Denman Street, I tried not to let my edits destroy the edgy quality of the writing.

The phone rang. "Pru," It was Rita. "There's someone here. Says he's an old friend. Wants to see you."

'An old friend.' Now who could that be? "I'll be right down." I ran a brush through my hair and put on some lip-gloss. 'An old friend.' 'He.' I could only hope it was an old childhood boyfriend who had found me again at last, or maybe Super Dan from Whistler had finally got tired of the lovely Barbara. Basically any man would be perfect if he could allow me to forget my infatuation with Charles Blackmore.

I ran down the stairs and into the restaurant. Charles Blackmore was standing at the cash desk, talking with Rita. *He's better looking than I remember. This is the first time I've seen him without a suit on. The aviator jacket, the gold-rimmed sunglasses perched on the top of his head, and faded jeans look great. Looks like he's been shopping. I wonder what's in that expensive looking boutique bag.*

I was about to race back upstairs to redo my make-up when they turned to look at me.

I was just starting to get over you, mister, but – -looking at you. Especially your hands. What is it about those strong, lean fingers? I felt nervous, excited. *Play it cool, Pru. You don't know why he's come.*

"What are *you* doing here?"

"I missed you, too." A wide grin spread across his face.

"Charles is someone I met while I was working in Aruba," I said to Rita.

"I came to deliver a message from Ovelia. She wants you to phone her. She has a surprise."

"Why'd she send you? She could have just called me."

Rita raised her eyebrows at the sharpness in my voice. Perhaps she was thinking it was a lover's spat. But, of course, it wasn't. *I haven't had the pleasure of knowing Mr. Blackmore intimately.* Desire seized my body. *Now, that is a shame.*

Blackmore checked his watch. "I want to see the look on your face when you hear her news. You can call now. It's only 9:00 pm in Aruba."

Rita said, "Why don't you take Charles up to your apartment, dear. We need the phone here for incoming reservations."

I'd never thought of Rita as an interfering busybody, until now, and gave her a look that told her what I was thinking.

"It's been nice to meet you, Charles. I hope you'll be around for a while," Rita said.

"I'm in town for a few days. I'd like to take all of you out for dinner tomorrow night. Could you get away from here for an evening?"

"Well, that would be just lovely, wouldn't it Pru? Your father would like to meet your friend."

I shot Blackmore a look of total annoyance, but his grin just widened.

I told you in Aruba that a relationship would never work between us. What are you trying to do?

"I'll make reservations at Mulvaney's on Granville Island. How's 7:00?"

"Seven will be just fine. Now you two run along and make that call."

I led him outside wishing I were wearing something more chic than a velour pantsuit. We began to climb the stairs where we encountered the ancient widow, Mrs. Porter, who lived down the hall. She was attired in a summer dress, a frock she would have called it, with ropes of pearls cascading across her droopy bosom.

"Miss Howard. How nice to see you."

She looked quizzically at Charles, but I wasn't going to give the notorious busybody the satisfaction. She'd have to see what information she could get from Rita.

"Going down for your afternoon tea, Mrs. Porter? Do have a good day." I kept walking up so she had no choice but to go down. We were left with the scent of sweet flowery perfume that she consumed by the liter.

Ella Fitzgerald and Louis Armstrong singing "The Nearness of You," greeted us as I opened the door. "We like the same music," Charles said.

"Forties jazz always seems to put me in the right mood to write." I tried to see my tiny apartment through the eyes of a millionaire. I wanted to be anywhere but here with him; the usual stack of newspapers and books littered the coffee table, and various edited versions of my current novel were lined up against the wall.

But I decided I'd have to be nice to him. We would be having dinner with him tomorrow, unless I could think of a way to get out of it. But, why was I trying to get out of it? I've wanted to sleep with the guy since I laid eyes on him. This could be my big chance. He says he'll only be here a few days. So just one passionate night and he'll be out of my life again. "Charles, would you like a glass of wine?"

"Love one."

I pulled a bottle of Chateau Simone from the wire wine rack. "Will this do?"

"That area around Nice is one of my favorite regions of France."

"Carlo introduced me to this wine." I put the tip of the wine opener into the cork and began to turn the screw.

"Here, allow me." Charles took the bottle. Our hands touched briefly and suddenly the room got warm, the space between us charged with electricity. I opened the cupboard and pulled out two oversized wine glasses. I willed myself not to be awkward. *Stay cool, Pru. Don't let him know how turned on you are.*

Charles poured the dark red liquid and handed me mine. We clinked glasses. "To remaining good friends," he said.

"To friends."

We sipped the wine; his eyes looked into mine, searching. If he was the least bit intuitive he saw, if not quite lust, an emotion verging on ardor. Okay. He saw passionate desire. There was no way to conceal it.

He lifted the glass from my hand and placed it on the

counter beside his own, then touched his lips to mine lightly, tentatively, "I *have* missed you," his voice husky.

His fingers moved softly down my hair, and then onto the back of my neck. Those hands I'd longed to be held by, folded me in an embrace; the musky smell of him exploding in my brain.

We kissed, softly, exploring the taste of each other. I touched the taught skin of his face and felt my fingers melt with desire. Everything disappeared except my body, his body. A glorious tingling feeling spread across my entire being. Then I was yanking off his leather jacket. We tumbled into the bedroom, stumbling as we tore off each other's clothing.

I've had sex hundreds of times, but nothing like this; the feeling of his naked skin touching mine, making my body respond to his every move. The longing in his eyes fueled my passion.

When our desire was satisfied he settled himself on his back, holding me against him. He seemed relaxed but my stomach was in knots. My body felt great, but my mind was saying 'Look out, Pru. Nothing's changed. If he finds out about your record with men, he'll be gone like a cool breeze.'

From the open window I heard the drip, drip, drip of a summer squall that had lashed rain against the side of the building.

"You know, Pru, I've wanted to make love to you since we first sat on Ovelia's porch. He blushed. "More after I saw you naked at Carlo's. I've never seen a woman with a more perfect body." It didn't seem possible, but his color increased. "But...well, there's something you should know about me."

Now, there is nothing worse than a guy making that statement after he's just had sex with you. Usually it's followed with a confession of being married or engaged or something of similar ilk. I held my breath.

He began to softly stroke the tops of my fingers and I could feel my desire for him returning against my better judgment.

"I guess by now you've realized that I don't like to beat around the bush. I'm a very busy man so I've learned to say what's on my mind."

"Well, say it, then. What is it you want to tell me?"

"I don't have girlfriends, Pru. I don't date women."

"What do you mean, you don't date women?" Here it comes, I thought. He's gay.

"I don't date." He turned his head to look at me, but I kept my gaze on the white expanse of ceiling. "You see, it's a long story...I grew up in a very ordinary middle-class home. But my buddies were from the wealthiest families in the city. In high school I got tired of being dumped for guys with cars and big allowances."

He turned over and leaned his head on his hand. I had to turn to look at him. His gray eyes seemed to be searching for some sign that I understood this kind of teenage angst. I did, but said, "Surely you have gotten over it by now." I had trouble keeping the sarcasm out of my voice. This kind of confession was not what I expected from the sophisticated Charles Blackmore.

"Childish I know, but it's been the driving force behind everything I've done for the last fifteen years. I decided I would make myself so desirable that no woman in her right mind would turn me down. The part I didn't foresee was that after I had acquired the wealth, I could never tell if a woman – and there seemed to be more of them than I could handle – liked me or the money."

"Some guys would kill for that problem, you know."

"Yes, you're right. But, women who knew virtually nothing about me except my financial status were constantly throwing themselves at me. It turned me into a cynic. So, here's the part you may not find so easy to understand." He let himself fall back against the pillows. He sighed and ran his fingers through his hair. "I wanted sex, so the easiest, simplest thing was to pay for it."

"Pay for it?" I felt my mouth go dry.

"I pay women to have sex with me. Very expensive, beautifully dressed women. That way I can have all the sex I want without having to let anyone in emotionally."

Gall rose in my mouth. "You think you can pay me to have sex with you." I grabbed the sheet and stood up, leaving Blackmore naked on my bed.

"No, Pru. You've got it wrong." He jumped out of the bed and stood in front of me, placing his hands gently on my arms. "That is the beauty of this. At first...when I was first attracted to you, I thought it was because you were the only woman I'd met who was making her own living. You were writing a book. You were working for Carlo. I knew you weren't having an affair with him, but you didn't throw yourself at me either. Do you have any idea how refreshing that was, by the way?"

I started to answer.

"Don't talk now, just let me finish."

I nodded and took a deep breath.

"Then Carlo told me about you. That you *had* come on to him because at the time you met him you were out of money. He was sure you would have slept with him, but what you probably don't know is that Carlo has never gotten over his wife. She died. He has no interest in having sex with any of the many women who cross his path. Then I had a talk with Ovelia. She let it slip that you lived with a series of quite wealthy guys."

He looked vulnerable standing there naked, so I wrapped the end of the sheet around him and maintained my silence.

"I have to admit that, at first, I was pretty disappointed. Instead of a woman I could admire, you were like all the rest. I fell back into my cynical mode. At least I tried to. But when I thought about you, and to tell you the truth, I couldn't get you out of my mind, I remembered the chemistry between us. I tried to push my feelings aside, but I couldn't stop thinking about you.

"I was still confused, though. I went back to England and visited with my mentor, Lord Pembroke. I told you about him. He's a man I really respect. He and his wife, Rachel, have had a long and successful marriage. He heard me out. I remember sitting in front of the fire in his library, him listening to my sad tale, as I then saw it, and chortling quietly after I finished. He said, 'Charles, I think you are finally in love.'

"He was right, of course. I told him all that stuff I said to you about how much I admired your independence. How I admired your morals. It was all nonsense, Pru. I mean, I do admire you. After all you are a very talented writer. But Lord Pembroke reminded me how I had used his position at Lloyd's to get into the shipping business. That he had lent me money *and* co-signed a loan when no one else would. When I saw that I had used him to get ahead, I knew that I was no different from anyone else. People do what they have to do to get what they want, and usually, like myself, they take the easiest road to get there. I could have worked and saved to get the money I needed. Instead, I used Lord Pembroke's generosity to move more quickly up the ladder. And he added one more thing. He said it was fine to make money if you didn't do any harm in the making of it." He turned his hands up in a pleading gesture. "You questioned me about that the night we met at Carlo's. Do you remember?"

I could feel a wry smile spreading across my face. "I let myself ask that question because it was something I was spending a lot of time thinking about. I shouldn't have had my mind on external speaker."

"No it was great that you did. You see, whenever that thought crept into my mind, I'd always justify it by telling myself that if I hadn't done it, someone else would have. But that's not a legitimate philosophy for anyone as self-righteous as I was being. All I have the right to say—honestly—is that I think I did more good than harm in all those places that were modernized by my containers.

"Anyway, that night in bed I tossed and turned until, finally near dawn, I realized I had been asleep. In that drowsy time before becoming fully conscious, I heard a sound deep inside me, like glass shattering. It was at that moment I let go of all the anger and frustration that I'd been holding onto for years."

Blackmore reached out with his hands in a gesture that could have been taken for pleading. "For a very long time I've felt superior to everyone else. I only hope that I haven't blown my chance with you by being so full of myself. You see, with Lord Pembroke's help, I saw I had to trust the chemistry. He said to me that day, 'Love is a verb. I love my wife. I have loved her for fifty-five years. And still, at times, she makes it very difficult for me to remember that I do. Times when I can't for the life of me, figure out why she is doing something just to annoy me. Those are the times I remind myself of my commitment to love her. And that means to do things for her. Sometimes they are not things I want to do, but things that will mean something to her. Because, Charles, my boy. That is what she does each day to put up with me. We are and have always been passionate about each other.'"

Blackmore moved forward so that he could wrap the sheet around both of us and once again took me in his arms. "But the most important thing he said was that if I saw you again, spent some time with you, well... I would find out if you want to love me, too. I swear there *is* chemistry between us. I'm tired of holding back my feelings. Keeping a woman at a distance so I can protect myself. Just now, making love to you, it felt good. Damn good."

"It might just be the thrill of opening up to emotion. Maybe it doesn't have anything to do with feelings for me."

"I don't believe that's true, Pru. But if you're worried about that, the only way to figure it out is to spend time together. See what happens."

I could feel myself reacting cautiously realizing that at one time, not that long ago, he did think I was using men, something he despised. Before I could stop myself, I said, "You don't know anything about me. We should just have sex for a while and then go our separate ways? No strings attached."

I could see by the look on his face that I had really deflated him, and it hurt me to do that. *Has this guy reached into your heart, Pru? After all, you have to admit that you've been pining for him for months now.*

"Look, Charles. You've really taken me by surprise here." I pulled away from him and slipped into my robe. "Just give me a minute to think." *Is this a guy I could actually love?* "I'll take back what I said a moment ago. I'll admit that in my own way, I'm as bad at this love thing as you are." I smiled at him and I saw his shoulders relax.

"There is a possibility that before now, neither of us met anyone we fell in love with," he said.

Possible. Probable, actually. I lived with men I knew I could never fall in love with because it was safe. Charles paid for sex. I, on the other hand, let men spend a lot of money on me. I traveled to the Far East with an Indonesian diplomat who I met in London. I spent time in Istanbul with a Greek exporter who loved to buy me jewelry. And then I traveled around Europe and went on that safari with Yves, the French wine exporter. Truthfully, I never went to bed with, traveled with, or took gifts from a man I didn't like...a lot. But I never kidded myself. I wasn't in love with, or ever would be in love with, any of them.

My way of retaining for myself a moral high ground was that when it became obvious they were really falling for me and would want to make things permanent, I let the bloom come off the rose by becoming difficult. I let them break it off with me to keep their pride intact. But should I admit the truth to Charles? I love being wined and dined.

I love nice things. It wasn't just being looked after while I wrote, I was living a great life, and I was getting laid. Charles has a great body, no doubt about that, but would I want him if he weren't rich? If he was a poor mechanic and we had to live off of my money...would I still want him? I ran my fingers along his jaw-line and felt the heat rise in me again. *Probably. As long as I had lots of money.*

"Charles, the reason my mother named me Prudence was that she hoped that virtue would rub off on me. She believed prudence to be the precondition of all the other values. She and I would ponder the question: *How can you act courageously if you don't consider the outcome?* When I choose to live with a man, my logic is always perfectly sound. Both parties get what they want. It could include love, but it doesn't have to. As long as everybody is having a good time."

"But if our feelings became love, would that be so bad?"

"I don't know. The last time I thought I was in love, I was in high school." I walked over to my dresser and ran my brush through my hair. Then I turned back to face him. "Like I said, I don't know much about it."

Charles moved closer and placed his hands on my shoulders. "I feel good when I'm around you. I want to go with that feeling. All those years when I thought I was protecting my precious heart, and my precious money, I hadn't met you yet."

"Oh." I looked into his eyes. Tears were forming. Actual tears. *If he's willing to be that vulnerable...*

He swept me up in his arms and carried me back to bed.

Now what? I asked myself as we lay holding each other. *What I do know is that every cell of my body feels alive when this guy is touching me.*

"You still have time to call Ovelia," Blackmore said into my ear. "I told her I'd be seeing you today. She said she'd wait up."

"Right. Okay." I leaned over and picked up the phone. "Do you remember the country code for Aruba?"

"297."

I leaned against the pillow, pulling the sheet up over my breasts. Blackmore laid his head on my shoulder, softly stroking my neck with the ends of his fingers, as I dialed Ovelia's number.

"If you keep doing that, I won't want to make this call."

The ringing stopped and Ovelia said, "Hello."

"It's Pru, Ovelia. Charles is here. He says you have something to tell me."

"I'm getting married. I want you to be here."

"Married." The image of Carlo holding Ovelia in the conference room came into my mind. I cringed. *She couldn't possibly still want that imposter. But hold on, Pru. This is her life, not yours. Whatever works. That's what you've always said.*

"You and Carlo will be very happy, I'm sure."

"Carlo? No Pru, I'm not marrying Carlo."

"Who then?" I sputtered. I looked questioningly at Blackmore.

"Christian. You remember, my friend the land developer."

Relief flooded my body. "Yes, of course I do. He's crazy about you. I could see that when we were in his office. But what about all that mushy stuff with Carlo? I don't get it."

"That's what Charles was counting on."

"Charles?" I looked down into his eyes, feeling my eyebrows rise. "What does Charles have to do with your love life?"

"The night after we had lunch with Charles at the Tortelli, when I got home, my boys said they had a job and could help me finance my new business."

"You do have the sweetest boys. They really love you."

"I know. But what you don't know is the job was working for Carlo. My sons were part of the group of kids catching the iguana."

"Oh my god. Really?"

"I wouldn't kid about that. Anyway, that did it for me. He did 'the thing' that turned my heart off. Remember the conversation we had about that? I called Charles and told him I'd counter-sue. We had a long talk about love, especially about my feelings for Carlo, which I came to understand were a form of paternal infatuation. He was a substitute for my father. Charles hatched the rest of his plan once I'd assured him I didn't want to spend my life with Carlo or hopelessly pining for the man. He was pretty sure that with Carlo's stock falling and with the threat of the counter-suit, Carlo would dismiss his case and return to Italy. Charles knew that you were disgusted with Carlo and that you would be just as disgusted with me if I played the lovesick woman. And you were. I was laying it on thick with Carlo and you were giving him such dirty looks, it clinched the deal. Carlo believed that because of my feelings for him, I would drop my countersuit. He stopped his lawsuit, shut down his Aruban company and hurried back to Milan."

"Well, you two are quite the con artists. Why should I believe anything either of you say to me ever again?"

"Because we both love you. Now Pru, are you coming to my wedding?"

I registered the fact that Ovelia said 'we both love you.' And it felt good. "Yes, of course. But isn't it a bit rushed? I mean you only just got together with Christian." I bit my lip. Here I was again suggesting someone take the time to think things through when it's not what I do.

"Actually, we went to school together. I know all about him. And the best part is that he knows all about me and still wants to marry me." Ovelia's soft laugh sounded over the phone. It was obvious she was very happy. "He adores my boys, too. Says he probably wouldn't have liked the baby stage but is quite willing to take on three youngsters. What more can a girl want?"

"You're right. What more can a girl want."

"Just for you to be here November 15th."

"I'll be there, Ovelia." I hung up.

"Well Mr. Blackmore. Why *should* I believe anything you say?"

"Aren't you supposed to believe in the man you're dating?"

"Dating?"

"Yes, we're dating."

I rolled the word around in my mind and found that I liked the sound of it. "Well then, tell me what happened to Carlo. Did you have your office spies check on him, too? Or do they only spy on women?"

"Usually just you, but I did make an exception in Carlo's case." Charles relaxed his hold of me. "I'm starving. Let's get dressed and go out for a steak. I'll tell you about Carlo over a glass of wine."

Dating? I think I like you, too, Mr. Blackmore.

The dank smell of ocean at low tide filled the air as we crossed the street to the English Bay Café. My friend, Bethany is the hostess there and when she saw me walk in with the gorgeous Mr. Blackmore she gave us the best table in the house. *Well, what are friends for?*

We sat on the banquette side by side, gazing at the sun setting through fast moving clouds over the bay as a large sailboat was heading into False Creek. Its crew was busily tying the blue sail covers onto the boom, while a small powerboat headed out for a sunset cruise. I sipped my wine.

"Okay. Tell me what happened to Carlo."Our Caesar salads arrived. "About Carlo, Charles."

"Ah, yes." He dug his fork into the lemon wedge and squeezed juice onto his salad, and then wiped his fingers on the starched napkin. "I realized that I could make some money while Carlo was learning to be a bit more compassionate."

"Money. I don't get it." My old suspicion about a businessman never missing an opportunity to make money, rose up.

"I hadn't set out to do this, but when the press got hold of the story of the green iguanas, Carlo's shareholders started to bail. I knew that wouldn't last for long. He's too good a designer. In time, and not much time at that, the public would forget about what he had done and start buying his shoes again. Meanwhile, I bought up the stock after the share prices fell. I even considered gaining control. But, then, he would know it was me, and to tell you the truth, I like Carlo. I think the whole iguana thing, including the lawsuit, was really a lack of judgment, not intentional malice on his part. He has quite a bad temper at times, but on the whole he's a decent sort. In fact, when he got news that the value of the shares was dropping he started to buy them back with his own money. His employees own a good deal of company stock; he pays bonuses that way. Carlo didn't want these honest, hardworking guys to have their retirement funds ruined."

"That *was* decent of him. You're right. Carlo is a good guy, really. He told me when I first met him that the workers in his atelier were like family. And he was very kind to me. Very generous."

"True, but I wanted to make him pay in some way for all the iguanas he killed. The night I went to the factory and saw the carnage..."

"I don't think anyone with a heart could have seen those creatures alive, enjoying the sunshine, and then wear them." I shuddered as I recollected what I had seen. The other memories from that time flooded through my mind. "But, how he went after Ovelia with the law suit. That *was* nasty."

"I know. If I were a Freudian analyst, which I'm not, I'd say that he's repressed his libido for way too long. All that pent up emotion had to come out somewhere and Ovelia was the unlucky recipient."

"I'll say. But how did you make him pay?"

"I sold the shares I bought, a little at a time, and as I said, he kept buying all the shares offered. It drove the price back up, so I made a healthy profit for my troubles."

"I don't know much about the stock market, but I thought you didn't want him to know you were involved."

"Oh, that's the beauty of the market. It's anonymous as long as I wasn't after control. He never knew it was me. Carlo was sure that one of his competitors was trying a hostile takeover. He was very worried there for awhile."

Two thick grilled steaks arrived smothered in pan-fried garlic and mushrooms. I picked up my steak knife and waved it under Charles' chin. "You don't deserve to live. You are evil and ruthless. Now I don't know who to feel more sorry for, Carlo or all those poor iguana."

"Actually, it's your fault, Pru."

"My fault? The stock play was your idea."

"You're the one who saved the iguana. Carlo and I have since decided that you deserve something for your part in all of this."

"Carlo and you? I don't understand."

"After I sold all my shares, I went to see Carlo and confessed."

"My god. What did he do? He must have been furious."

Charles reached over and handed me the boutique shopping bag that he had refused to leave in my apartment. "This is from Carlo. He wants you to open the letter first."

I remembered now that it was the same bag that the maid had brought to my stateroom on Carlo's boat. I opened the thick, creamy envelope embossed with Carlo's initials and unfolded the thick paper.

Dear Miss Howard,

There is no need for me to reiterate the anger I experienced over the iguana incident. I am grateful that has passed.

The first night you and I sat on my boat, I asked if you believed in angels. You said you were more a Jungian, rather than a traditionally religious person, if I remember correctly. As you know, I do believe in such spirits, the proof being, you brought me a message from my dear Angelita. (I have given Charles permission to relate the story of my wife to you.)

You see, I realize now that in spite of the fact I started Minelli Shoes to honour my beloved Angelita, the success of my atelier changed me. I became greedy for the power that success allows. I thought I could do whatever I wanted no matter whom or what was harmed. I believe that my Angelita saw this change in me and sent you to me to get me to mend my ways. Because of your courage to stand up for what you believe to be correct, I have been able to put my life back into balance. For that I am forever in your debt.

In order to show a small token of my appreciation, please accept another pair of red shoes. These, you will note, were made from the skins of domesticated cows. I vow never again to use wild animals for such purposes.

Secondly, after Charles explained what he had done to manipulate the value of my stock, and the consequent money that he made to really drive home this lesson, we decided to start a foundation in your name. Its purpose is to try to stop the extinction of the black rhino in East Africa.

It is the least I can do. You have truly given my soul back to me.

Respectfully,

Carlo

I folded the letter and placed it back in the envelope, and then took the shoes from the box. High-heeled sandals, as before, but these were made with the softest hide I had ever felt. When I put them on, they fit perfectly, as the others had. *I have to hand it to Carlo; he knows his stuff.*

I stood to let Charles see the shoes on my feet and watched his pupils widen as they do when men are aroused. *Thank you, Carlo.*

I sat down and stared into his eyes. "You and Carlo started a foundation? Really?"

"Yes. It was the best way we could think of to honour you and your commitment to wild life on the planet. But it comes with a personal request from me."

I felt my stomach lurch. *If something seems to be too good to be true, it usually is.* "What would that be?" I tried to keep my voice even. I didn't want him to see my disappointment. *Why does everything good always have a catch?*

"I want you to dedicate the next month of your life to me."

"Excuse me?"

"In the villa I own in Morocco. I think you would have an enjoyable time writing there. Morocco's where I got my start in the container business. I return to it as often as I can. The weather's wonderful in the winter."

"And what would you be doing while I wrote? It's a lonely business, writing. I spend hours thinking and reading and getting my ideas down on paper. It's not a spectator sport."

"One of my talents, known only to a few of my closest friends, is that I'm an artist of sorts. I paint when I get the time at my flat in London, but what I've always wanted to do is to take an extended period when I could do nothing else." He pushed his partly eaten steak away. "The truth is, Pru, I've worked too damn hard for the last fifteen years. I have money I can't spend and I have a highly trained staff that can run things without me for a month or two. I'd like to spend that time with you."

An ambulance siren screamed past. *It's either an accident victim or a senior citizen on his way out. Life's short, Pru. This man seems to like you, warts and all. The real truth is, you like him. Besides, you've learned he's not perfect either. And by starting that foundation, he's proved that not all businessmen are evil as that professor believed.*

"Morocco?"

"Yes. Have you been there?"

"I have, as a matter of fact. I understand the appeal. It's colorful, exotic, and warm...but..."

"Look, Pru. You may as well tell me. I'm a novice in the relationship department, but it seems to me that if we are going to make a go of this, we have to tell each other what we're thinking."

I cut another piece of the tenderloin. *Yup, if you really want the steak and not just the sizzle, Pru, he's right.* I put the meat in my mouth and chewed. It was great. Juicy. Savoury. *Go on, Pru. You want a relationship you can describe that way and this man might just be offering you one. Maybe you will finally be getting what you need. You always decide things quickly. Just go for it.* "Well, the truth is, I can't be in Morocco. I almost caused an international incident the last time I was there."

"You did? This I've got to hear."

"I'd already seen the overloaded donkeys, and the rail-thin horses being struck on their back-bones, and then I came upon an Arab who was beating his donkey. I lost it. Started yelling at him. I don't think he understood a word I was saying, but he certainly knew what I was upset about. Then, when he didn't stop, I grabbed the switch out of his hand and smacked him with it. My boyfriend pulled me away just as a policeman was walking over to see what all the fuss was about. I can't stand the way they treat their animals. It drives me insane."

"So you don't want to go."

"Apart from being with you." *Oh, my god, Pru. Did you say that out loud? You did, because he's smiling.* "Could we go somewhere else?"

"We can, and we will. I wouldn't want to run the risk of you ending up in a Moroccan jail. How about Florence? They use modern vehicles to do their farming. We could even take some Italian cooking classes. That is when we're not eating in one of their great restaurants."

"When do you plan to do this?"

"Now. I've already arranged to be away for the month."

In three days Dad and Rita were leaving for Britain and I would be looking after the fish and chip shop. I took a large gulp of wine to steady myself. "I can't go."

He stiffened. "Can't or won't?"

I covered his hand with mine. "Can't. My father and Rita are leaving for Britain in three days and I'm looking after the restaurant. Could we go some other time?"

I saw his shoulders relax. "I want to be with you now. Especially after this afternoon. I told you before that I'm aggressive about getting what I want. I convinced myself that you'd want to be with me, so I arranged my schedule to have this time. After that I have a series of meetings set up with the ruler of Brunei. He's not someone I can casually call to change the meeting time."

I remembered the apartment next to mine. Rita used it as a vacation rental during Expo and it was vacant now. I was supposed to interview possible long term renters. I was pretty sure that Rita wouldn't mind waiting on that for a month. My apartment was small, too small to include a man like Charles, but I was sure we could survive a month together if he had his own space in which to paint. We could see how much we wanted to be with each other the rest of the time. "How would you feel about staying with me in Vancouver?"

As soon as I put the question to him, I felt light. I could be the host rather than the guest. I didn't need him for any reason other than just being with him. That was completely new for me. This was the second time in a few weeks that the money I earned was giving me a deep sense of self-respect and I liked it.

Charles picked up his glass and offered a toast. "Let's drink to Canada."

Acknowledgment

I am deeply grateful to have an editing group of women who remain as devoted as I to the writing process. Their comments and suggestions were invaluable to this book. They are: Lynda Crawford, Marlyn Horsdal, Sharon Bronstein, and Helen Hinchcliff.

I also appreciate the time that four other women devoted to the reading and commenting on the completed manuscript. Sheila McEachern, Susan Lee, Gillian Campbell, and Margaret Stuart all gave me important feedback and suggestions.

To Tracy, my daughter-in-law, whose excitement after reading the manuscript inspired me to work to make it the best book of which I was capable.

Thanks to my daughter, Samantha, and her daughter, Uma (my granddaughter) for providing the cover photo. They and my other granddaughter, Layla have from the beginning been supportive of my writing efforts.

And finally, to my husband Richard Weatherall who inspires me daily with his lively, thoughtful conversation. He saved me from the technical parts of the publishing process to which I, alone, would have surely failed. Words will never be enough to express my gratitude.